I0690954

AIRSHIP 27 PRODUCTIONS

Aviation Aces
"Rescue" © 2018 Gene Moyers
"Windy City Widow" © 2018 Jeff Fournier & Andy Fix
"Missing in Malaysia" © 2018 Robert Ricci
"Operation Blow-up" © 2018 Fred Adams Jr.

Published by Airship 27 Productions
www.airship27.com
www.airship27hangar.com

Interior illustrations © 2018 Howard Simpson
Cover illustration © 2018 Shane Evans

Editor: Ron Fortier
Associate Editor: Kaushik Karforma
Marketing and Promotions Manager: Michael Vance
Production and design by Rob Davis

ISBN-13: 978-1-946183-47-7
ISBN-10: 1-946183-47-4

Printed in the United States of America

10 9 8 7 6 5 4 3 2 1

Volume One
TABLE OF CONTENTS

Rescue
Gene Moyers

T he view from five thousand feet was breathtaking. The sky was cloudless and from the front seat of the Lockheed float plane Luke Lance could see to the horizon more than 20 miles away. He glanced over his shoulder to the rear cockpit. Jerry Burns lolled back in his seat his face turned to the sky. Luke couldn't see his eyes behind the tinted goggles but it wouldn't take much to imagine them closed as Jerry enjoyed the sunshine. Luke knew better though; Jerry was too good a flier to doze off when they were on a job.

Luke shifted his glance down and to the right. There, two thousand feet below the huge Empire Class flying boat thundered along. Its four powerful Pegasus engines were driving it north toward Singapore across the Java Sea. Luke knew they were making good time. The big flying boats were fast. They cruised at 160 knots. That's why K.O. had given them the Lockheed. It was one of the few aircraft the Agency had that could escort the big flying boat. She made a proud sight her light grey hull silhouetted against the dark blue sea.

Glancing at his watch, Luke noted that they were still three hours out from Singapore. The trip had gone smoothly with no sign of trouble. They had seen no other aircraft and the flight was on course and on time. Still, the airline had engaged the famous *Straits Agency* to fly security and it was Luke and Jerry who had drawn the assignment. Luke shrugged. It looked like they would earn their money easy today. Besides it meant a chance to fly the Lockheed, one of the sweetest aircraft the Agency had.

His eyes sweeping the horizon suddenly focused ahead and Luke sat up straight. There, ahead was a tiny speck. It could have been nothing more than a bug strike on the wind screen but he knew differently. As he watched it grew larger. Within seconds he knew it was an aircraft on a direct course for them. "So much for a milk run," he thought to himself as he spoke into the intercom, "Heads up Jerry. We've got company."

Behind him he could hear and feel as Jerry swept the Lewis gun around on its circular mounting, "Roger, I see him, Ten o'clock high and closing to port."

Luke cursed and jerked his eyes skyward. Sure enough another speck was closing on them, this one a couple of thousand feet above them. Two of them, just great! He spoke again, "We'll take the high one first." He pushed on the throttle and brought the stick back. The Lockheed responded and seemed to leap upward. The unknown plane grew rapidly larger. Soon Luke could make it out as a two seat monoplane on floats painted light blue. He didn't recognize the type off hand and didn't have time to study it as they closed.

The blue plane was in a shallow dive toward the flying boat. When it seemed to hesitate and swerve in its dive Luke knew they had been sighted. The plane curved toward them and the range closed. A thousand yards turned to five hundred quickly. Four hundred, Luke reached for the charging handle and jerked it back, arming his guns. Three hundred yards. He itched to open fire but he still didn't know if this plane was truly hostile. Two hundred yards away the blue plane swerved sharply to the left. Surprised for a moment, Luke ducked involuntarily as tracers arched from the rear cockpit toward them. He squeezed the trigger and the twin thirty caliber wing guns in the leading edge spat fire at the bandit. He was over him, his tracers flashing just above and behind the bandit.

Pushing the stick forward he dove after the bandit snapping off short bursts. He was getting the range but his aim was thrown off by the bandits skidding flat turns. He was doing this to avoid Luke's fire but the maneuvers also unmasked his rear gunner to fling lead at them. Finally Luke got in a burst that tracked through the enemy's tail. Desperate, the enemy pilot threw his aircraft on its back and dove for the sea. Surprised that the bandit's floats didn't tear off at the sharp maneuver Luke pushed down the nose of the Lockheed and dove after him. As he did Jerry's voice came over the intercom. "Luke, the other plane made a pass at the flying boat but now he's broken away and he's headed this way!"

"Got it," Luke gritted out as he banged on the throttle to get more speed. He needed to wrap this up quickly before the other plane got in range. He closed in slowly. The enemy's rear seat gunner had stopped firing: either he was out of ammo or he was reloading. Luke fired again. As he did he heard Jerry open up with the rear gun. He didn't waste time looking over his shoulder; it would just scare him. Instead he continued walking his fire in. The bandit's rear gunner must have reloaded because more tracers floated out from the rear cockpit toward the Lockheed. He felt the plane vibrate as enemy fire hit them somewhere. Luke stayed focused; he kicked in a little right rudder and walked his fire along the rear fuselage and through the tail.

Jerry had been firing continuously and as the bandit in front of them faltered Luke heard him scream, "Reloading!" Fabric was fluttering off the bandit's tail from his rudder as well as the elevators. The enemy pilot had throttled well back and it was obvious he was having trouble controlling his craft. Enough; Luke hauled the Lockheed into a steep bank. As he did he chanced a glance over his right shoulder. The bandit turning toward them was a green painted monoplane with retractable landing gear. Great! That meant it was probably faster and more maneuverable than the Lockheed. Slamming in left rudder Luke skidded the big floatplane to the left as tracers drilled through the air where they had just been. Jerry fired and yelled, "He's coming around again!"

Sweating hard now, Luke jerked his aircraft around strongly to the right and nearly collided with the closing monoplane. He flashed past so quickly neither pilot had a chance to fire. Luke kept his plane in a steep bank attempting to get around behind the green plane. The bandit broke right and also went into a steep bank. Now both aircraft were in vertical banks flying on opposite sides of a huge circle in the sky. Each aircraft was at full throttle attempting to get behind the other. Knowing that banging on the throttle would get no more speed from the upgraded Wright Cyclone engine Luke glanced up. Free of drag the bandit was faster, as he had suspected. Slowly it was gaining on them. Another couple of turns and it would be able to pull lead on them and that would be it.

Making a decision, he jerked the stick to the right and back and plummeted downward. Luke heard Jerry curse as he struggled to get the wings level. When he finally did they were going steeply downhill fast; doing well over 200 knots. Looking back Luke could see the bandit had been surprised but was in fast pursuit. He yelled to Jerry, "Are you reloaded?"

"Yep, just give me a shot," came back the quick reply. Good old Jerry, Luke knew he could always depend on the cheerful Mick, especially when things were going south.

"Okay, he's going to be behind us pretty quick. Hold your fire but point your gun straight up. Got it?"

"Straight up? Are you...uh, got it."

Luke eased the throttle a bit and twisted his head to watch the closing aircraft. It grew bigger quickly. He could feel the cold sweat running down his forehead but he stayed calm. He continued to wait. Just as he thought the bandit was in range he yelled out, "Standby!" and jerked the stick back all the way into his stomach. The Lockheed immediately went into a steep zoom climb. As he held the stick back she started into a loop. Tracers from the bandit flew through the space where they had just been. Every rivet straining the big float plane groaned as Luke kept the stick back. It came over the top; the bandit passing two hundred yards below it, now going the opposite way. For a brief moment it passed directly through Jerry's sight. He didn't hesitate.

He held the trigger down and walked a long string of bullets down the bandit from nose to tail. As Jerry ceased fire Luke rolled the Lockheed level and cut his throttle back. He looked over the side and could see the bandit going down. It was in a spin, obviously out of control. Luke put a wing down and circled lower watching it spin toward the sea. Just before it hit, the wings came off and there were three tiny splashes three thousand feet below.

Luke took the Lockheed down to a thousand feet. It didn't take long to find the damaged float plane. It had landed safely but was in trouble. It was listing and deep in the water. The pilots had scrambled out onto a wing and stood looking upwards as the Lockheed swept low toward them. Thinking they were about to be machine gunned one of the pilots leapt into the ocean. Jerry's laugh came over the intercom, "Suspicious bastards, aren't they?"

Luke replied, "Probably what they would have done to us if they got the chance. Did you see where the flying boat went?"

"They cracked the throttle wide and headed northwest, probably half way to Singapore by now."

"No use trying to catch them now. I guess the airline's fears about a hijacking were right. I wonder what they were carrying that was so important."

He could almost hear Jerry's verbal shrug, "We'll probably never know. But we saved their bacon, that's for sure. Hey Luke, look out to port. There's a boat closing on us."

Luke glanced down. There was a dilapidated fishing boat steaming past below. It was headed straight for the downed float plane. He told Jerry, "Probably working with the aircraft. They force the flying boat down and up comes the boat with men to loot it while they fly cover." Luke smiled as they turned for Singapore. "It might have worked too if we hadn't been riding shotgun."

☆ ☆ ☆

Three hours later Luke brought the Lockheed in low across Singapore harbor. He cut the throttle and dropped the sleek aircraft gently down on the water. She skimmed the waves and bounced once before settling and sliding across the murky water. He taxied toward the quay leased by the agency and cut the engine. An agency mechanic tossed them a line and pulled the Lockheed the last few yards. Once moored at the quay,

Luke released his seatbelt and climbed out onto the wing. He stretched and jumped down to the quay. The first thing he did when out of the plane was to unzip and take off his leather flying jacket. He needed it while flying but Singapore harbor sweltered under the usual humid heat. He turned back to the Lockheed but all he could see of Jerry was his legs and backside as he bent into the rear cockpit. Luke could hear muffled curses and a moment late Jerry popped up carrying his precious ukulele by the neck. He examined it carefully as if it were a small baby. Luke smiled and asked innocently, "Is she alright?"

Jerry glared at Luke as he jumped to the quay, "No thanks to you. She got thrown around pretty good but I think all she picked up was a couple of scratches." He strummed a couple of notes, listening critically, "I think she's okay." Luke shook his head; Jerry and that uke were inseparable. He glanced at where Jerry was pointing. Along the fuselage behind the cockpits was painted *The Straits Agency*. There were now three round holes through the 'r', the 'g' and the 'y'. He looked a Luke, "Close."

Luke punched Jerry lightly in the bicep and smiled, "Good shooting. You really stitched that buzzard."

Jerry nodded as the two walked up the quay towards dry land, "You know that it's not possible to loop a floatplane, don't you? Or do Immelmann turns, for that matter. I thought that the floats were going to come off...and the wings too."

Luke threw his head back and laughed, "It seemed like a good idea at the time. Besides we didn't have a lot of other choices." He shrugged, "She held together okay." Jerry nodded toward the figure striding toward them, "Tell it to K.O. I'm sure he'll have something to say about abusing his precious ships."

Kendrick Owen Pike was the millionaire owner of the *Straits Agency*. He had a strong six foot frame and a voice to match. He was a gifted pilot, a sharp business man and strong-willed enough deal with bureaucracies, governments and greedy merchants. He had built the Straits Agency into a successful flying detective and security agency famous all over Southeast Asia. They flew gold, tracked criminals and would haul anybody anywhere at a moment's notice. With branches in every city from Bombay to Peking they were also respected by most governments in the region. Now he was striding toward the two tired pilots, his corn cob pipe clutched in his teeth and streaming smoke like a locomotive.

As the tall figure neared them K.O. pulled his pipe from his mouth and boomed out, "So you two flying pirates made it."

Jerry pretended to look offended. Luke just raised a hand in greeting,

"Yeah, we made it, a little the worse for wear. Did the flying boat make it in okay?"

Shaking each of his pilot's hands, K.O. nodded, "Yep, it landed nearly an hour ago. I guess you two put on a pretty good show for the passengers."

The two pilots smiled weakly. "It was some show alright," Jerry modestly admitted. K.O. fell into step with them. Luke looked curiously at him, "I guess you were right that she was in danger. Where did you get the info?"

K.O. replied, "The airline came to me with reports that their Empire boats were being shadowed by unknown aircraft. Since they were planning a valuable flight they hired us to provide security." He clapped the two pilots on the shoulders, "You two did a great job. The airline manager here has already been to my office praising you two. Go clean up and get some rest. Jerry I want to see you in my office tomorrow afternoon. Luke I've got something for you as well. Be in my office first thing the day after tomorrow." Giving them each another friendly clap on the shoulders he strode away yelling for his maintenance chief.

Jerry smiled and shook his head, "I don't know about you but I could use a beer."

Luke agreed. "I'm buying."

✩ ✩ ✩

Two days later Luke was knocking on K.O.'s Singapore office door. At the gruff command to enter he opened the door and went in. Tossing his hat onto a file cabinet he sprawled in a comfortable chair across the desk from his boss.

K.O. his jacket off and sleeves rolled up in the heat did not look up from his writing, "Don't get too comfortable Luke. You're flying today."

Luke perked up at his news, "What have you got for me K.O.?"

K.O. put down his pen and looked up, "Search mission."

Luke thought about that as he watched K.O. use a pen knife to clean out his corn cob pipe. "Searching for what?" he asked.

"I had a Mr. McKnight in here recently. He's the local manager for International News Service. It seems that one of INS' correspondents has gone missing and he wants us to make a private search effort. I'm putting you in charge of it."

Luke frowned, "Okay. When do I start, and who am I looking for."

You're looking for Sandy Clawson. She went missing off the north coast of Sarawak a couple of days ago. I want you to get out there right away. I'll send more planes as they become available. I'm afraid we're a little short of people right now."

"Luke frowned, "A skirt? What was she doing running around out there? Just a lot of reefs and empty islands, and you know if she's down in the sea there's not a lot of hope for her and her pilot."

"It seems that INS had her out trying to track down some biologist who's doing studies of birds for National Geographic magazine for an interview. Her plane was overdue two days ago. I want you to fly to Sarawak today. Go up to Miri and start searching." He stood up and handed some folded maps across the desk, "I've marked out the areas where she was searching for the biologist."

Luke took the maps, "Who was she flying with? Anybody I know?"

"As a matter of fact, she was flying with Roy Cavitt. You know him, don't you?"

Luke stared, "I sure do. I met him up in Hong Kong when I was working for the Nanking government." He thought for a moment, "Roy's a damned good pilot. If he was flying the girl her chances just went up. Roy would have got them down safe if anybody could."

K.O. nodded, "Well, I hope we find them both safe and sound. Better get over to the airfield. They're fueling up your ship now. I'll be out before you take off."

Luke stuffed the maps in his pocket ant reached for the door, "What am I flying?"

"The Waco."

"The Waco? Why can't I take the Lockheed? It's a float plane and I may need one if I'm searching the sea for them."

K.O. had sat back down and picked up some papers, "Can't have it, Jerry took the Lockheed up to Saigon last night. Ben Cowan needs him up there."

"Isn't there anything else?"

K.O. gave him a stern look, "And what's wrong with the Waco?"

Luke shook his head, "Nothing per se. It's great for ferrying tourists around, but it can barely get out of its own way."

K.O. looked annoyed, "Listen, hot shot. You're not going out to do any stunt flying. This is about search and rescue. The Waco's a cabin job with lots of room for rescue gear and passengers. I'm having the rear seats taken out and an extra gas tank installed to give you more range."

Luke protested, "We're gonna have a heck of time working the guns out the side windows with all that cargo."

"You're not going to need any guns. I told the boys not to mount them. And you're flying alone. I hope to send Sam tomorrow and Jerry when he gets back from Saigon to help you." Luke looked unhappy. K.O. continued, "You're taking the Waco because that's all I've got. Now get out of here. I've got work to do." He turned back to his paperwork. Luke left and didn't care that the door slammed harder than it should have.

He took a taxi to his apartment and had it wait while he changed into flying clothes. He then took it out to the commercial airfield. At the *Straits Agency* hangar things were busy even though the Waco was the only aircraft in sight.

The Waco was a biplane cabin job. It was a stable plane that could haul four passengers and luggage. It was sturdy and dependable, but not very fast. The Waco would probably do more than a hundred and twenty five knots; and that was downhill with a tail wind. Luke shook his head and headed toward the knot of men working on her.

The head mechanic came over to him wiping his hands on a rag, "Hey Luke. We're just buttoning her up now. She'll be ready to fly in a few minutes," he jerked his thumb over his shoulder where two mechanics were lifting a cowling back onto the engine. Luke nodded and walked over to peek into the cabin. The rear seats had been removed as K.O. had said. Instead there was a large metal tank bolted in their place. There was also a lot of other gear in place. Most of it packaged in canvas packages. He turned to the mechanic, "How big is that tank?"

"Fifty gallons, it ought to give you a lot more range."

Luke nodded, "What's all that other stuff?"

"K.O.'s orders. There's a lot of survival gear. Food, tools, signaling equipment. If you find the dame and can't land, you can drop them some stuff to hold out until you can bring in more help."

Luke nodded and wandered off to a safe distance where he could light up a cigarette. It seemed like he would well equipped. Too bad he wasn't flying a hotter plane but K.O. was right. The Waco would work out well for the search. With two more planes joining him soon they should be able to cover a lot of area. With a little luck they would find Roy and this skirt and bring them back in one piece. He finished his cigarette and was lost in thought when the head mechanic waved to him.

He helped them roll the Waco out onto the field and he started his pre-flight inspection. When he was happy she was in good shape he climbed

"What's all that other stuff?"

aboard and turned the engine over. The Wright radial engine fired up immediately and settled down into a smooth roar. Luke nodded; she'd been tuned up just fine. At that moment a car turned the corner of the hangar, and stopped and out stepped K.O. He held out his hand and raised his voice to carry over the idling Wright engine, "I wanted to wish you luck, Luke. I'll get you some help out there soon. Take care of yourself."

"Thanks K.O., I'll do my best." Luke turned and climbed into the Waco. He tightened his belt and with a quick wave gunned the Waco forward. Steering with the brake pedals he taxied rapidly to the runway, waited for a clear space and revving the engine shot forward. With flaps the Waco was airborne in a surprisingly short distance. Luke climbed, circled the field once and set course eastward. Watching the Waco dwindle until it was speck, K.O. didn't turn away until it disappeared.

Once in the air, Luke climbed to five thousand feet and set course due east. It was just over four hundred miles to Kuching. At cruising speed it should take about three and half hours to reach the capital of Sarawak. He settled back to enjoy the flight. The sky was crystal clear with unlimited visibility. He had checked the weather before leaving Singapore and they had told him there were scattered squalls moving in from the north in the next few days. Luke's flight was uneventful and he landed at the Kuching airfield soon after one o'clock.

At the Strait's Agency hangar, the Waco was checked over and refueled while Luke checked in with customs. In less than an hour he was on his way again. He set a course running northeast along the coast. Sarawak's coast was sparsely populated and heavily forested here in the southwest. The coastal area north of Brunei was more populated. Luke would be operating out of Miri near the border with Brunei. He reached Miri before five o'clock. After making a good landing he was waved over to an empty hangar by a coverall wearing figure. He taxied up to him and cut the engine. The prop wound down and jerked to a stop as a figure came over and opened the cabin door, "Captain Lance? I'm Fred Jones. Your company wired me that you were coming in today. They've hired my hangar and told me to give you any help I can."

Luke nodded, "Good. I'm gonna be leading a search for a possible downed plane?" Jones nodded, "You're looking for Captain Cavitt and that lady reporter he was flying around, aren't you?"

Surprised, Luke questioned, "You've seen them?"

"Yep, I refueled and checked over his plane when they were in. They were searching here for uh, lemme see…three days before they didn't come back."

"You don't know where they were searching do you?"

The mechanic shook his head, "Not exactly, north of here somewhere. That pretty lady reporter told me they were looking for some kind of bird scientist. I think they started looking at islands along the coast. After that…" he shrugged. Nodding to himself Luke told the mechanic to fill up the Waco and get it ready an early start tomorrow. He also got him to telephone for a local taxi to take him into town.

Early the next morning Fred had the Waco warmed up and ready to go when Luke arrived. A quick check of the aircraft and Luke taxied out and took off into the wind. He headed north and climbed to three thousand feet. That was high enough to give him a wide view but low enough to make out small craft such as life rafts. Consulting his map Luke began the tedious flying involved in a search. Every island or large reef needed to be overflown and given a good look. Every shiny reflection in the sea that could be a mirror signaling had to be checked out. It was slow work. After four hours he wished for a co-pilot to spell him at the controls. Early in the afternoon he turned back for Miri. He had Fred refuel the Waco while he grabbed a quick lunch and soon he was headed north again. The afternoon was the same boring search work. He overflew several small islands but found no sign of encampments or downed aircraft. The sun was low on the western horizon when he turned for Miri. He set down soon after dark. Turning the Waco over to Fred he thumbed a ride into town to the cheap room he had rented.

The next day was a repeat of the first. He shifted his search area to the northeast and found more small islands but still no sign of any down aircraft. After a long day of tedious searching mile upon mile of ocean, Luke returned bone weary to the small airstrip at Miri. Fred was waiting for him, with a telegram. It was from Kuching and dated that day from Sam, another Agency pilot. It stated that he had arrived safely but his aircraft needed work and he would not be able to reach Miri until late the next day. Luke shook his head, another day of searching alone. He left the Waco in Fred's hands and went to look for something to eat.

On the third day Luke moved his search area north. He was now working toward the very tip of northern Sarawak. There were many more small islands here. Some of these islands became a chain that ran north into Philippine territory. These islands were in a kind of no man's land that had been disputed between Spain and Sarawak in the last century. For the first time in the search weather became a factor. Instead of clear skies and unlimited visibility Luke was finding scattered clouds with dark thunderheads coming in from the north. Some of them were dark pillars that towered thousands of feet into the air.

Consulting his chart Luke swung around to northeast. There were some small scattered islands he wanted to check out. Unfortunately, the dark clouds were moving fast in that direction as well. He pressed on hoping to reach the islands before he had to return to Miri for fuel. The sky got darker and the air rougher. Luke was rethinking his decision when suddenly rain began falling. Rain fell hard and it grew dark very quickly. Soon he was flying nearly blind. He put the nose down and tried to get under the soup. Depending on his instruments he herded the aircraft lower and lower.

Luke finally broke out into relatively clear air at five hundred feet. The air was rough and he was still battered by strong wind gusts. Orienting himself he had just decided to turn for home when he caught sight of a dark mass to his right. Kicking in right rudder he came around and made out the dark green form of a small island. He decided to scout this last island before turning back. Putting on some speed he climbed carefully.

Visibility went to zero as he climbed through a thousand feet and a rain shower hit him. He could see the island briefly then lost it in dark clouds. Luke was jerked hard against his seat belt as he hit a down draft. He fought the stick for control as he shoved hard on the throttle for more power. Two minutes of hard struggling later he broke through into clear air. Looking around he could see the thunder shower behind him, ahead was scattered white clouds. Looking down and to the left he could see a small island covered in vegetation. Beyond it about a mile was another larger, hilly island also covered in vegetation. He brought the nose around and headed for the small island.

Luke was checking his fuel gauge when he caught a flash of light high and to the right. His head came up as an aircraft emerged from a towering cloud bank. Startled Luke saw a small biplane heading directly for him. The aircraft was a thousand feet above him but closing fast. It was unusual to meet an aircraft out here in the middle of nowhere. With a bad feeling in his stomach, Luke banked away from the unknown aircraft. The unknown pilot was being awfully aggressive; it was closing at high speed on a collision course. Luke banked right and put the nose down while keeping an eye on the strange aircraft. It was small, painted dark gray and carried no markings. There was something familiar about it Luke decided as it continued to close with the Waco. Deciding he wanted nothing to do with this strange aircraft Luke looked for the nearest cloud blank.

The gray plane swept closer at frightening speed. With no cloud cover nearby Luke instead rolled to the right and pulled the stick back sharply throwing the Waco into a dive. It was a good thing he did; as he winged over tracers flashed through the space where he had just been. Luke cursed and pulled his wings level. Looking back, he saw the bandit pull up sharply into a loop. At the top of it he rolled his wings over and turned it into a full Immelmann. He then rolled into a screaming dive straight at Luke.

Luke shoved the throttle forward. Whoever was flying that crate was good. And that was no civilian plane; he had seen ones like it before. The bandit rapidly closed the range as Luke waited. As the bandit swept in twin nose guns sparkling he threw the Waco to the left. He felt and heard a rattle against his tail as if a handful of gravel had been thrown at it and knew he'd been hit. He didn't know how badly but the controls felt alright as he turned in and under the enemy. The bandit banked sharply around as it came around again to get on Luke's tail.

Luke cursed his lack of rear vision as he craned his neck around trying to see where the bandit was. He kicked the rudder left and right to see behind him. It was good he did as tracers flew past. He felt a couple more hits as he threw the Waco into a bank cursing loudly, "Won't need any guns, eh! Simple search mission, eh!" He would have some things to say to K.O. if he got back to Singapore in one piece.

The gray biplane used its higher speed to climb above the Waco. At three thousand feet it dove fast and opened fire at four hundred yards. Luke saw him coming. He couldn't do anything but wait until the last second and as the tracers walked past his nose he dove. He heard metallic bangs as bullets hit his cowling. The bandit flashed past and pulled up into a zoom climb. It circled and came around to get behind the slower Waco.

Luke recovered at a thousand feet. He had the throttle wide open but the Waco's engine was missing. One of the bandit's bullets had hit something. He glanced at the gauges. Oil pressure: okay, temperature: okay. Luke grimly pictured a bullet hole through one of the pistons. With his speed below a hundred knots he was going to be easy meat for the bandit who was again circling around behind him. Luke could see the smaller of the two islands a couple of miles to his left, the larger island beyond. Maybe he should try to put it down on the island. It beat being shot down into the sea.

He shoved the side window back and craned his head out. Behind him the bandit was curving around behind the damaged Waco. Running out of options Luke decided grimly that if he was going out he was taking that

S.O.B. with him. He pulled back the throttle and cranked in some flaps. The Waco slowed. He kept his head half out the window his eyes fixed on the enemy plane. It was closing fast now. Luke stayed focused. The Waco was very stable. Its twin wings gave it plenty of lift even at low speeds and it had large lower wing flaps. That was his play.

The bandit was doing two hundred knots in a shallow dive as it opened fire. As the first tracers flashed out, Luke yanked the throttle all the way back and frantically cranked in full flaps as he yanked the stick back with his other hand. The Waco lost speed and bounced upwards as the flaps took hold. Closing too fast, the bandit suddenly found the Waco bouncing upwards into his path. The pilot hauled frantically back on his stick as the Waco filled his windscreen. It was close enough for him to see the face of a man looking out a side window. At the last second the enemy pilot jerked the stick to the left attempting a wildly tight run to avoid striking the biplane.

Luke watched frozen as the bandit closed with him. As he got within yards his aircraft reared like a frightened horse and then fell off on one wing; its wheels seeming to brush across the Waco's left wingtip. Luke watched as the stalled enemy plane fell into a spin. There was less than a thousand feet of air below the two aircraft now. The bandit didn't have any chance of recovering. Luke watched it all the way in. There was no sound but he clearly saw the white splash as it crashed nose first into the sea.

Luke turned his attention back to the wounded Waco. His speed was down to seventy knots. He pushed in some throttle and cranked the flaps back to the halfway mark. The engine was still running rough. He pulled the nose around toward the smaller island and sank toward it. The island was flat and less than a mile across but heavily forested. The only clear space was on south side. A small clearing led from the beach inland. As he neared it Luke could see it was covered in long grass and small bushes but looked flat enough. The bad thing was; it was only a few hundred yards long.

With no the choice Luke lined up on the clearing and came in from seaward. Five hundred yards out he cut his engine switches. The prop slowed and it became very quiet. He cranked in full flaps and sank slowly down. The waves got closer and closer. Luke knew he had to come in as low and slow as possible or he was going to run out of clearing and end up in the trees. Speed was down around fifty knots as Luke skimmed the shallows and spray flew up from his wheels as he hit the beach in less than a foot of water. He crossed the beach in a second and was bumping through rough grass. Small bushes and saplings tore at the lower wing as he rolled inland. He was slowing but not enough. Suddenly the tail of an aircraft appeared in the bushes. He pushed right brake with his foot and swerved around the wreckage but the trees were only twenty yards ahead. He was still doing about fifteen miles per hour when he stepped down on the brakes. The Waco nosed down hard. The tail came up and very gracefully it nosed over gently into a mass of bushes. It came to rest nose down, the tail sticking up at an angle of more than seventy degrees.

For a moment Luke hung from his seat belt stunned. As the tail had tipped upward, packs gear and other loose items in the cabin had rained down around him and wound up resting against the windscreen. He reached to his left and unlatched the cabin door. Gravity pulled it downward. Carefully bracing his free arm and feet against the forward bulkhead Luke released his seat belt and fell against the control panel. He leaned outward and tumbled from the plane. Shakily he got to his feet in the tall grass and looked around. He had come to a stop just twenty yards from the trees. To the left of the plane he could see the tail of a downed aircraft one wing sticking into the air. He shook his head as he walked toward the other plane, "They say any landing you can walk away from is a good landing."

He reached the other plane in seconds. It was a two-seat monoplane, and badly torn up. He looked toward the beach and could see by the torn grass and brush what had happened. The pilot must have done the same thing Luke had. He came in low across the beach and up into the clearing. Unfortunately, a hundred yards in he must have hit a rock in the grass. It had torn off his landing gear which Luke could see sticking out of the grass. That had spun the aircraft around into a ground loop and it had wound up tilted up on one crumpled wing.

As Luke approached the monoplane he could see a number of small holes peppering the tail and rear fuselage. Grimly he estimated they were probably the same size as the bullet holes in the Waco. Climbing up on the fuselage he looked into the rear cockpit. It was empty but there was dried blood everywhere. Flies disturbed from feeding buzzed around his head in a cloud. The forward cockpit was empty. On the other side of the wreck he could see a mound of earth in the grass. Jumping down he stepped over to it. The six-foot-long low mound of earth must be a fresh grave. Sobered Luke decided a grave meant survivors. Deciding against an immediate search, he trudged back to the Waco.

After doing a walk around Luke decided it wasn't too badly damaged. There were a few bullet holes in the tail but structurally everything looked intact. The wings had been cushioned by the low bushes when she nosed forward and the prop looked unharmed because he had cut the engine before he hit. The only thing that worried him was the engine. If the engine was shot it wouldn't matter about the rest of the plane.

Luke took off his jacket off. As he turned to the cabin a crashing of branches caught his attention. He spun around, his hand reaching for the .45 in his shoulder holster as a figure crashed out of the forest ten yards away. He caught a glimpse of blonde hair before the figure tripped face forward into the tall grass with a sharp cry. He reached the girl just as she pushed herself to her feet. She was of medium height. Her blonde hair was matted and there was a piece of brush caught in it. One sleeve of her khaki shirt had been torn; her breeches were dirty and torn. What he could see of her face was attractive and she certainly filled out the filthy shirt.

Before he could say anything, the girl wiped her hair out of her face and gasped, "Thank God!" She licked her lips and asked, "Do you have any water?"

Nonplussed Luke jerked his thumb over his shoulder, "Back there…"

She staggered past him. He turned and grabbed her arm as she tripped and led her to the Waco. Once there she collapsed gasping for breath. Digging around in the cabin he found a canteen and handed it to her. She grabbed it and drank gratefully, water spilling out the sides of her mouth. She lowered it and closed her eyes and whispered, "Thanks, I really needed that."

In a moment she seemed to have regained her wits. She stood shakily and said, "I don't know who you are but I'm damned glad to see you. I ran out of water two days ago." She looked around, "Uh, just who are you anyway?"

"I'm Luke Lance and if you're Sandy Clawson, I'm here to rescue you," Luke said brightly. The girl looked surprised and then glanced around. She took in Luke's somewhat battered appearance and the tilted Waco. As she brought her eyes down from the tail high in the air she looked skeptically at him, "Rescue? Mister I think you need to work on your rescue technique."

Trying not to be annoyed Luke replied, "I was doing fine until some clown started putting bullets in my airplane," he waved his hand at the Waco's tail. "I found you didn't I. What happened? Is that Roy's grave over there?"

The girl looked sharply at him, "You knew Roy?"

Luke nodded, "I flew with him up in China. Good flier. What happened?"

Sandy sat down wearily, "We'd been searching islands along this coast for several days when we spotted these two. As we got close enough for a look a plane came out of nowhere and started shooting at us. Before I knew what was happening Roy was hit and the engine was dead. He managed to put it down in this clearing but we hit something and crashed." Her eyes teared up as she looked at Luke, "I tried to help him but there was blood everywhere. He said a few words and then just died." Luke wanted to say something but wasn't sure what. He had lost friends before and there never was anything comforting to say. Instead, he asked, "What happened then?"

She shook her head. "I passed out after that; shock I guess. When I woke up I wandered into the jungle to look for help but I didn't get far before I heard a motor boat pass by. This island is pretty small. I beat it back here but I found three guys with guns climbing around our plane. They searched Roy's body and then took some stuff from the plane and just left. They didn't even try to bury him. Jerks!" She paused, "I buried him with a small camp shovel I found in the plane; thank god those guys didn't take it with them. I've spent the last few days here trying to survive. I ran out of water two days ago. I couldn't have lasted much longer." She hung her head and Luke realized she was exhausted.

He stood up and paced around, "Where did those men come from?"

She shrugged, "The other island I guess. Couldn't have been anywhere else."

Luke looked thoughtful, "If they saw you crash, they probably saw me. We'll have to keep an eye out." He turned and began digging around in the Waco until he found a small bag of tools. Opening it he grabbed a screwdriver and went to work on the engine cowlings. He had to stop and pull some brush out of the way but soon had one of the cowlings off. He was peering inside when felt someone at his elbow, "What's it look like?"

His head down, Luke replied, "Not too bad. It looks like a bullet cut through one of the spark plug wires. That's why she was missing so badly. I don't see any other obvious damage." He pulled his head back and looked at the girl, "If I can cannibalize a wire from your plane and there's not any other damage we might be able to get this thing in the air again."

The girl looked skeptically up at the tilted tail, "Are you sure?" Standing up Luke dusted his hands off, "Sure, the two of us and some rope ought to do it." He started pulling packs out of the Waco. Opening up a few of them he found what he was looking for: rope and a hand axe. As he handed her the rope he asked, "So what do I call you?"

"Call me Sandy."

"Luke." Hefting the axe he set out for the forest. She followed along. "So, who were those guys with the guns; pirates?"

He gave her a look, "Pirates don't fly Kawasaki fighters." When she frowned at him he continued, "I spent a lot of time in China flying for the Nanking government. I've seen those fighters before. The Japanese are phasing them out now for their new Nakajima monoplanes but they're still pretty hot birds. I was lucky to get away from the one today." He stopped at a small sapling with a trunk two inches across, "This ought to do." He cut it off at the ground and then used the axe to strip all the branches off for about six feet where the trunk formed a Y. He cut it there and started dragging it back toward the plane.

"What's that for?"

"We'll use it to ease the tail down to the ground. Then I can make better judgment about the engine." When they reached the plane, he positioned the cut tree under the tail and motioned Sandy to hold it. He then picked up the rope and flipped it up across the tail. "Okay, now hold that branch steady. I'll pull the tail downwards. When gravity catches it, it'll fall into the Y of the branches. We'll then ease the branch slowly backwards and the tail will come down gently." Sandy looked doubtful. Luke smiled, "Trust me, and hold that branch steady."

Taking up both ends of the rope he pulled slowly. The tail wavered and then dropped backwards. The Y branch was positioned about halfway along the fuselage. The tail dropped about two feet and landed solidly but fairly gently into the Y. Luke smiled as he grabbed the branch, "Now we'll just walk it back." They dragged the ground end of the branch backward. As they did the tail dropped lower and lower. Finally, the branch was angled out at perhaps thirty degrees holding the tail about four feet off the ground. Luke motioned the girl to stand back and kicked the branch sharply with his boot. It flew off into the grass and the Waco's tail dropped to the ground with a thump. Luke bent down to examine the tail wheel. The ground here was soft and the wheel seemed to have absorbed most of the impact.

Luke then went back to work on the Waco. He got the other cowling off and after a quarter hour pronounced the engine sound except for the cut plug wire. Grabbing a couple of tools, he set out for the wrecked monoplane. Once there he managed to get a cowling off and dig around the engine. With a little bit of work, he removed a complete spark plug wire without damaging it. He then trudged slowly back to the Waco. Sandy had discovered some food and was chomping away happily as he returned. He

The tail wavered and then dropped backwards.

held up the plug wire and smiled. Sandy smiled back but before she could speak they both heard it; the sound a throbbing engine. Sandy had gone had gone pale. "It's them!"

Luke took off running toward the beach. He stopped a hundred yards from the sea and listened. Sandy came panting up behind him. They could both clearly hear the engine but could see nothing. Luke grabbed Sandy's arm, "What did they do the last time?"

She pointed at the beach, "They landed there. Three of them got out and walked up to the plane. When I saw the guns, I stayed in the jungle. They didn't look for me. They must have thought Roy was alone." Luke pulled her toward the forest and into the trees, "They'll see the empty plane and know someone's here this time. Keep still now."

The two crouched down behind trees and waited. A minute later a boat came into sight. It was about fifty yards off shore cruising along the south end of the island. As soon as the men in the boat sighted the clearing they nosed their craft toward shore. It was an open boat about twenty feet in length powered by an outboard motor. A man sat in the stern steering it. Three more sat forward. Luke could see that two of them held rifles. He took Sandy's hand and pulled her with him as they eased back. Staying in the tree line they moved northward watching the boat as they went. The man in the stern steered the boat onto the beach and cut the motor. Three men jumped out, all with weapons. Two of them men had rifles; the third carried a cumbersome looking weapon. Luke and Sandy moved inland through the trees to a point opposite the damaged Waco. Luke whispered in Sandy's ear, "They'll make for the plane to search it. I need to surprise them. Stay under cover, okay." Her face pale, Sandy nodded.

Luke ran crouched across the clearing to a spot near the Waco. He flattened himself behind a large bush about twenty feet from it and waited. Minutes later he saw two figures approaching up the clearing from the beach. They were tanned, roughly dressed and wore battered, wide brimmed hats woven from native plants. Luke decided they might be Malays although one of them looked like he had some oriental blood. They approached the Waco cautiously, rifles up and calling out to each other softly in some native dialect. Once at the aircraft they excitedly pointed to the scattered gear. One of them turned and peered into the Waco's cabin. The other one squatted down to examine the loose gear.

The moment right, Luke came to his feet and threw himself toward the squatting man. Startled he stood up and tied to bring his rifle up. Luke brushed the rifle barrel aside with his left hand, shoved his .45 into the man's chest with his right and pulled the trigger. The gun went off but not with a bang; instead the sound was muffled by the man's body. He went flying backwards to sprawl on his back. Luke jumped his falling body and hurtled toward the other man who had spun around. Before he could bring his rifle up Luke was on him.

Luke dropped his gun, got both hands around the man's throat and squeezed. The man dropped his rifle and tried to pry Luke's hands from his throat. They struggled like that for a moment. The man's face began to turn purple. Suddenly he let go of Luke's hands and snatched a long-bladed knife from his belt. Luke let go the man's throat and grabbed for the knife hand. He got both hands on it. The two struggled silently for a moment; the only sound the man's gasping breath. Gradually Luke turned the knife back toward his opponent. The man's eyes bugged out as he realized what was about to happen. Luke kicked a foot out from under him and they crashed to the dirt. They rolled around for a moment and were still. Sandy ran forward to help but the men were already on the ground. They stopped moving and she thought for a moment that both were dead. Then Luke groaned and pushed himself to his feet. The knife stuck straight up from the dead man's chest.

He stood there for a moment breathing hard, then picked up his .45 and holstered it. Sandy asked in a tiny voice, "Are you alright?"

Luke nodded as he picked up the man's dropped rifle. He looked the weapon over and frowned at it. Sandy whispered, "What do we do now?"

Luke looked at her and spoke quietly, "We have to get that boat before the other two guys figure out what happened." He reached down and put one of the men's hats on his head. He turned to Sandy and said, "I want you to walk in front of me with your hands up. They'll be watching you. That will get me close enough to use the rifle. When I yell, you hit the dirt, okay?" She bit her lip and nodded.

They marched through the grass and scrub toward the beach. Sandy had her hands up and Luke stayed close behind her. As soon as they were sighted by the men at the boat, someone called out to them. Luke kept his head down but waved an arm casually. They kept walking. Someone called out again. Luke saw that one man was in the stern of the boat the other was on the beach holding a heavy looking weapon. He judged they were about eighty yards away. He took a breath and yelled, "Down!"

Sandy dove forward into the grass. Luke threw the rifle to his shoulder and took aim, praying the sights were correct. As he did the man fired his strange weapon from the waist. Luke fired just as a burst of automatic fire blasted from the weapon, the bullets flying just over his head. Luke worked the bolt and ran forward. The man on the beach was down. The man in the boat was frantically trying to start the motor. Luke fired at him and missed. Cursing he dropped to one knee, took a breath, let it out and fired again. The man stiffened upright and fell over the gunwale into the surf clutching his chest.

Luke worked the bolt again and walked down to the boat. It was empty. A roughly dressed man floated in the surf face down. He walked back to Sandy who stood near the downed shooter. She looked very pale as she stuttered, "Are they all..." Luke nodded. Sandy covered her mouth and turned away. Luke shook his head and knelt to examine the dead man's weapon. It was three and a half feet long and had a strange ringed barrel. There was a bipod folded up under the barrel and an odd boxlike attachment on the left side of the breech. Most interesting it had a strange, swooping combination butt stock and pistol grip. Luke picked it up and hefted the weapon. He had seen these before but he had never actually lifted one. It was surprisingly heavy; he decided it must weigh nearly twenty pounds.

Sandy, still pale but under control came up at that moment. She frowned, "What kind of gun is that?"

Luke looked thoughtfully at her, "This is a Japanese Nambu light machine gun. It's the standard Japanese squad machine gun. I saw a lot of them in China." He set the weapon down and picked up the rifle. He worked the bolt and ejected a cartridge onto the sand. Picking it up Luke added, "This rifle is a Japanese Arisaka. It fires 6.5 mm cartridges the same as the machine gun. You remember I told you the biplane that shot me down was Japanese?"

Sandy nodded. She then frowned as Luke began searching through the dead shooter's pockets, "He doesn't look Japanese." The man was Caucasian. The contents of his pockets were no help; cigarettes, matches and a few British pounds.

Luke agreed, "No, and the two back by the Waco aren't either. But something fishy is going on." Lifting the man's arm Luke hissed, "Ahhhh." Sandy leaned in and saw a tattoo of a snake on the inside of the man's wrist, "What's that?"

"A tattoo," He let the man's arm drop and stood up.

Sandy hugged herself and asked, "What do we do now?"

Luke shrugged, "I'm not sure, but we can't stay here for long."

Sandy said brightly, "We have the boat now."

Luke shook his head, "Too small, we won't get far in that. And they'll wonder what happened when these guys go missing." He looked thoughtful, "We need to get the Waco going if we can, but it's almost dark." He waved a hand at the setting sun and continued, "I don't know how much I can get done in the dark and there'll be more guys over here by morning."

He rubbed his chin thoughtfully, "You know we might go take a look at that other island. They must have larger sea going boats. Maybe we can steal one; or a plane. They must have some kind of airstrip over there too." Sandy looked interested at this. She nodded, "I'm game for that." Luke looked suspiciously at her but then shrugged, "Okay let's get moving."

In the fading light they made quick preparations. Sandy disappeared into the forest and returned with a sack. It contained the few possessions she had salvaged. From it she pulled a small camera and snapped a couple shots of the Japanese weapons. While she did this, he checked the wrist of the other two gunmen. They each had the same snake tattoo. Luke gathered up all the ammo he could find on the dead men and also brought along a pair of binoculars from the Waco. They took the time to eat a quick meal to give the sky time to darken thoroughly. Lastly Luke gathered up the Nambu and loaded it into the boat with them. Pushing the boat off the sand they clambered in, started up the motor and steered the boat westward.

They had crash landed on the south side of their island. He guided the boat around the west end and headed north. The larger island lay about a mile north across the dark sea. Luke didn't have a compass but could make out the darker form of his destination against the lighter sky. The island appeared totally dark with no signs of habitation. When they reached it, Luke started a slow circumnavigation of it. They slowed to idle periodically to listen but heard and saw nothing. After an hour they had worked around to the north side of the larger island. During a period of listening Luke heard what sounded like an engine start up. The sound was distant but distinct. Looking at Sandy he could see she had heard it also. They motored slowly forward. Soon Luke made out a break in to tree lined shore. At first, he thought it was a narrow bay but as his eyes adjusted to the gloom he realized it was the entrance to a lagoon. Overshadowed by large trees, the entrance was no more than thirty yards wide. More interesting Luke thought he could detect a dim glow from somewhere deep within it. He turned the boat around and motored a half mile back along the northern shore where he cut the engine and let the boat coast onto a tiny beach.

Wading ashore Luke dug the small anchor into the sand and helped Sandy out of the boat. Whispering in her ear he said, "I think whoever it is has a something going on in that lagoon, probably where they keep a bigger boat.

We'll approach from the west and check things out." She nodded. He gave her the binoculars and his .45. They divided the rifle cartridges in their five round clips and he hefted the Nambu onto his shoulder. Before they set off Sandy grabbed his arm and whispered quietly, "Before we go any farther. Tell me about those tattoos. You recognized them, didn't you?" Luke lowered the gun to the ground and leaned in close, "I've seen them before. There's a shadowy figure here in the islands. He's known as the Viper. He's supposed to be involved in everything from smuggling to white slavery and everything in between. Nobody knows exactly who he is or where he operates from but every major police force and government out here would like to get their hands on him. Supposedly his men have a viper tattooed on their forearms."

There was a sharp intake of breath from Sandy, "The same tattoo?"

"The same. I think the Viper's got something going on here. What I'm really interested in is where he's getting all these Japanese weapons from. Are you still game?"

She nodded silently. Luke hefted the gun and set off carefully through the forest. Though heavily forested there was little underbrush and they moved fairly easily. After fifteen minutes or so of traveling they stopped to rest. As Luke lowered the gun to the ground they both heard it; music. They listened for a few minutes while catching their breath. Soon the music stopped but started up again moments later. Sandy whispered in Luke's ear, "A record player?" He nodded and moved off slowly carrying the Nambu.

Minutes later they stopped again. The music was louder now. Setting down the Nambu, Luke got down on his knees and crawled forward. Sandy wriggled up beside him and they both crawled forward the last few yards to the edge of a clearing. Sandy hissed quietly at the sight before them.

The ground ahead had been recently cleared. Tree stumps were everywhere. The clearing was dimly illuminated by several oil lanterns hung from posts and buildings. They illuminated the western edge of a dark lagoon. A dock had been built on the shore nearest them. Across the lagoon a steep hill ended in a cliff overlooking the dark waters. Moored at the dock was a good-sized boat. A dim lantern hung on her stern and a light came from the pilot house. Luke reckoned her to be at least fifty or sixty feet long, probably an ocean-going fishing boat from her looks. She would have range of hundreds of miles. Up from the dock where she was moored was a large, open-sided building. In the gloom there appeared to be stacks of crates piled there. Several other tiny to medium sized building were scattered around the west and south sides of lagoon. There were a few people out and about. While they watched a man left one of the tiny shacks, a privy Luke judged, and headed toward a larger building with light and sound coming from open windows. Every person they saw moving about seemed to be male.

Luke and Sandy wiggled back to the Nambu. "Wow," she whispered in his ear, "Jackpot!" Luke grabbed her arm, "Just what's that supposed to mean?"

There was a pause, "Well, it's kind of what I was looking for."

Luke raised an eyebrow in the darkness, "I thought you were looking for some bird scientist out here somewhere."

Her voice sounding a little bit guilty, Sandy continued, "Yeah that was the story. My news service has been getting reports of strange goings on in the South China Sea. Both the British and the Dutch military have been sighting unidentified submarines in this area, and several ships have gone missing. So my news service sent me out here looking for some kind foreign activity. I was to scout around for strange ships or aircraft. I guess this Viper guy you were talking about is behind it all. This must be his secret hideout."

Luke was silent for a moment then shook his head, "Wrong; this place is new. Couldn't you tell? Those tree stumps were fresh. So was all that construction, new wood if you look close. No, there's something else going on here. C'mon." He turned to go then stopped. He leaned in close to her face, "If you'd told Roy this he might still be alive."

Stung, Sandy whispered harshly back, "Once we were out searching, I did tell him what we were looking for. We were both shocked when that plane started shooting at us." Her voice broke with a sob, "I didn't expect anything like that." Luke felt guilty. He patted her on the shoulder, "No crying, sound carries, C'mon." He set off again moving carefully.

Minutes later they again emerged from the trees. They had come out onto a cleared path. Luke oriented himself; they were south of the camp. The path ran south past the base of a small hill and wound south through more trees. The hill was bare except for scattered small bushes. The path was wider than a foot path. Chances were that it had been cleared for carts. Luke motioned Sandy after him and started up the hill. From there he should have a good view of things. Staying low and using what cover they had the two soon made it to the crest of the small hill.

The few trees on the hill had been cleared to give a wide view from the top. There was also some kind of structure there. He immediately crouched, Sandy ducking down a moment later. They heard and saw nothing and moved up carefully. The moon was just rising in the east and in the dim light but it took Luke a moment to realize what it was.

It was a circular group of sandbags perhaps eight feet across and three feet high. In the middle, silhouetted against the rising half-moon, was something metallic. In the poor light it wasn't until Luke was right up against the sandbags that he realized it was in fact a large gun. He leaned the Nambu against the sandbagged wall and stepped over it, immediately tripping over one of the gun's low tripod legs. He caught himself on the nearly five-foot-long barrel and almost whistled in surprise. He kicked something metallic and looked down. Around the inside of the sandbagged walls were metallic boxes. He bent down and tried to move one but it felt as if it nailed to the ground. He found a catch, popped it upwards and opened the box. Inside were a series of heavy metal magazines. He held one up in the weak moonlight. Bright metal gleamed inside. He moved around the gun to what was obviously some kind of shoulder rest and a pistol grip.

All this time Sandy was standing by the sandbags watching him. Finally, no longer able to hold her curiosity she hissed at him in a low voice, "What is that thing?" He held his finger to his lips and stepped back over the sandbags and crouched down. Sandy crouched down beside him. He spoke quietly, "That is an anti-aircraft gun. It's Japanese, maybe one of their 20mm or 25mm guns. This is serious stuff. You don't find something like this on the black market. The Viper must be dealing with the Japanese in a big way."

Sandy whispered, "This gun is impressive as hell but I was talking about that thing down there under the cliff."

Luke looked surprised. He stood up and peered over the gun down the hill. It took a few seconds but finally he recognized a dark shape up under the cliff that bordered the east side of the lagoon. He pointed at the binoculars slung around Sandy's neck and she handed them to him. It took a minute to focus the glasses on the base of the cliff. Moving the glasses slowly Luke realized that the cliff had been under cut and a narrow quay had been built against its base. The most shocking thing was what was moored against the quay. Barely visible in the shadows was a submarine. It was dark but Luke could barely make out a dim glow coming from the conning tower, probably light leaking up through the deck hatch. After a bit he saw a brief flare of light on the forward deck. Watching a shape move, he realized someone had lit a cigarette. He quickly sat back down behind the sandbagged wall as he felt a pull on his arm.

Sandy stared down into his face, "Well? What is it?" Luke handed her the binoculars and said, "A submarine." She stood up to look, froze and sat back down, "A what?"

"A submarine, I can't tell what kind. Even in daylight I'm not an expert on ships but I'm betting it's probably one of the smaller Japanese subs." He smiled wryly up at her, "I guess this explains all those rumors you were chasing. It looks like the Japanese are working with the Viper. They must have paid him to help set up this secret base. That's why his men have all these modern weapons."

Sandy let out a deep breath, "Wow! Do you realize how big this is? Stories like this come along once in a lifetime." Her voice had risen slightly and Luke had to shush her. He whispered back, "Do you realize what this means to the British, the Dutch, the Americans, everybody? If war comes, the Japanese have a secret base deep in the South China Sea. This is an act of war."

Sandy hissed back, "Right, we have to get this story back to Singapore, right away."

"Uh huh. Have you forgotten we have no transportation?"

Sandy slumped back against the bags, "Oh yeah, what are we going to do?"

"We keep on and find that airfield. If we can't steal a plane then we take a look at that boat. It's getting late and when everyone settles down we might be able to pull off something." While Sandy digested that, he carefully stood up behind the gun and used the binoculars to scan the camp. When he sat back down he handed the glasses to Sandy and picked up the Nambu. He then set off down the hill to the south with Sandy close behind.

They reached the base of the hill and continued south. They followed the wide path a couple of hundred yards through the trees before they reached the edge of a wide clearing. Crouching down behind a tree Luke looked carefully around. The clearing was in fact the east end of a narrow airstrip that had been cut from the vegetation. He could make out canvas tents about halfway down the strip along the north side. Light leaked out through seams and people moved about. One large tent had the sides rolled up, was illuminated and Luke could clearly see an airplane with several people around it. He motioned and Sandy silently handed over the binoculars. Luke focused on the aircraft. It was a Kawasaki biplane fighter just like the one that had tried to kill him earlier. The cowling was off and two uniformed mechanics were obviously working on the engine. As Luke watched another uniformed Asian came over to the mechanics, spoke to them, looked over the plane and left. Luke handed the glasses back to Sandy who took a long look.

Finally, she whispered, "You were right. It's a plane. Can you fly it?"

Luke nodded, "Yeah, the problem is it's a single seat fighter. Gonna be tough squeezing you in with me. Besides they're working on it. Let's watch a while." They settled down behind the tree watching. They took turns using the binoculars. They saw what were obviously sentries passing by the tents and eventually they saw the mechanics pin the cowlings back on the Kawasaki and retire to a tent. Looking at his watch Luke saw that it was nearly midnight. The half-moon was now high in the sky providing a good bit more illumination. Luke motioned Sandy further back in the trees. He then whispered, "The plane's no good. There are too many guards and people around."

"What about the boat?"

"Before; I thought we had a chance to steal it but the submarine changes everything. If we got away with the boat they'd just come after us in the sub and sink us. I think we've got to sneak back to the boat and get back to my plane. We have to hope we can get it running and take off tomorrow before they come looking for their buddies. They must be worried that their boys aren't back by now."

Sandy mulled this over, "And if you can't get your plane working?"

"We stay in the jungle and wait for help. My boss is going to be upset about his missing plane. He was already promising more help to search for you. Now there will be a bigger search. I think things are going to get hot for the Viper's men here as well as those Japanese soldiers."

Sandy looked startled, "What Japanese soldiers?"

Luke smiled, "Didn't you see those guys in uniform by the plane? The viper's men were all wearing civilian clothes. Those were Japanese mechanics and pilots. And you can bet that sub's crew is Japanese too."

"Oh," she said in a very weak voice.

Luke picked up the Nambu and turned just as an armed sentry walked through the trees and saw them in the moonlight. Luke rushed forward. The sentry lowered his rifle and lunged at him, the long bayonet attached to the rifle gleaming in the moonlight. Luke used the Nambu to block the first thrust but it was too heavy to use effectively. The sentry gave out a cry and lunged again. Luke blocked another thrust but tripped and fell backwards. The sentry loomed over him with his bayonet raised. Luke reached for his .45 and remembered he had given it to Sandy. A shot rang out. The sentry dropped his gun, reached for his back and collapsed next to Luke. Luke scrambled to his feet and yelled, "Thanks," as he grabbed up the Nambu. Sandy stood there looking shocked as he brushed past her to the edge of the runway.

The sentry loomed over him with his bayonet raised.

Dropping to the ground Luke unfolded the bipod and took a grip on the machine gun. Snugging it against his shoulder he sighted down the airstrip and opened fire. The heavy Nambu didn't really kick much. Luke fired another burst at the dark shape of a tent. Although he couldn't hear them because of the ringing in his ears, people were screaming. He could see the people boiling out of the tents and he snapped out short bursts at them. He must have hit something in one of the tents because there was an eruption of flame and the tent up like a torch. The gun ran dry. Luke cursed and reached for his pocket.

He hadn't realized that Sandy had flopped down beside him until she shoved a five-round clip of ammo into his hand. Luke fumbled at the hopper attached to the left side of the weapon and dropped in the clip. He repeated this five more times as Sandy passed clips to him. He jerked the bolt back and opened up again. By the light of the burning tent he could see the fighter plane and he concentrated his fire there. He could see dirt kick up from his bullets all around the plane. A half-dressed man rushed to the plane and was caught in Luke's fire and collapsed to the ground. Luke the put more rounds into the fighter until his gun ran dry again.

Abandoning the gun, Luke stood up and shoved Sandy into the trees yelling, "Run!" Behind them there was chaos. People were screaming and blindly-fired bullets were flying around. They located the path and ran north toward the lagoon. Ahead they could see lights and hear lots of noise from the camp. Suddenly Luke swerved off the path and pulled Sandy with him. In a loud whisper he said, "We have to get to that gun!" He put his head down and pushed through the trees and brush. Sandy sputtered, "What? What do you…" Finally, she just cursed and pushed after him.

A minute later they came out at the south side of the hill. To their left they could see lights moving past them on the path to the airstrip and hear shouted voices. Luke turned to Sandy and held out his hand, "Gimme the gun." He took his .45 from her and started climbing the hill, Sandy puffing along after him. "Why don't we just run for our boat?" she pleaded. Over his shoulder Luke replied, "It's not going to do us any good unless we can knock out their boat, otherwise they'll just sail over and shoot us. We gotta stop it to buy time.

Nearly winded Luke reached the top of the small hill with Sandy close behind. He vaulted over the sandbags as Sandy huffed, "What do you want me to do?" Luke pointed down, "Open up those metal boxes and get out a magazine." As he spoke he was doing just that himself. He had plenty of light to see. In addition to the moonlight, the whole camp was lit up. Lanterns and hand lights flashed all around the camp and he could see people running around. Across the lagoon shielded lights had come on above the submarine. Sailors were scrambling around on the deck and Luke could see exhaust smoke at her stern. Someone had started up her diesels.

Fumbling one of the heavy magazines up, he placed it on top of the gun's receiver. It took a few seconds to get it lined up and he cursed under his breath before it snapped into place. He jerked back the heavy bolt with a metallic 'clack' and was reaching for the trigger when Sandy yelled. Running up the hill were two men with guns. They were no more than twenty yards away. They saw Luke at the gun and raised their rifles. Snatching his .45 from his holster he snapped off four shots and the men tumbled away. He tossed the gun to the shocked Sandy and followed it up with a spare magazine from his pocket. He leaned against the shoulder rest and swung the gun toward the fishing boat. As he reached for the trigger he shouted to Sandy, "Cover your ears!"

At three hundred yards the boat filled the sight. He squeezed the trigger lightly and the big gun went off with a crack that echoed across the lagoon. The first round was a tracer and it flew into the stern of the boat. Satisfied Luke squeezed and held down the trigger. Every fourth round was a tracer and it was easy to direct his fire. There was surprisingly little recoil. The heavy mount absorbed most of it. It was more of jolting against his shoulder as he walked his shots up the length of the boat. Splinters, glass and dust flew everywhere. As the gun clicked on empty, Luke saw several men dive overboard into the water. He jumped forward and wrenched out the now empty magazine and turned to pick up another. Sandy stepped forward and handed him one. She was struggling with the nearly twenty-pound weight and Luke took it from her gratefully.

With a new magazine in place, Luke swung the gun toward the moored submarine. He aimed for the conning tower and fired once. His tracer flew over it and hit something sticking out the top. He lowered his sights and began firing quick single shots at the sub. He could see flashes as every time as the copper jacketed shells hit the subs iron hull. He had fired perhaps fourteen or fifteen rounds when he saw flashes out of the corner of his eye. Sandy was down behind the sandbags firing his .45 down the hill. He swung the gun around and saw a knot of men with guns running up the hill. He opened fire down the hill. The gun's shells ripped up the earth throwing dirt and rocks up all around the men. A couple of them threw themselves to the ground; the rest dropped their weapons and ran in all directions. Luke burst out laughing. The gun empty he pulled out the magazine and bent down for another. He got the magazine in place and looked over at Sandy. Her mouth was moving and she was holding up the .45, its slide locked back. He shook his head realizing he couldn't hear a thing she was saying because of the ringing in his ears.

Reloaded; Luke swung the gun back to the lagoon. There was now a small fire burning in the boats superstructure and men running toward the boat. He sighted on them and opened fire. His shells tore up the dock. Men jumped from there into the lagoon. He swung the gun toward the buildings and fired again. Then he saw movement. The sub had cut its lines and was moving slowly toward the lagoon's entrance. Luke swung his gun toward it and sighted again on the conning tower. He fired and hit it. Men on it ducked somewhere as Luke continued firing. Suddenly the gun clicked on empty and Luke looked around. The sub was still making for the entrance to the lagoon but Luke had hit it hard. Something on top of the conning tower was canted over at an angle. There was a fire burning on the after deck of the fishing boat. One of the buildings was on fire as well. He turned to grin at Sandy. She was yelling something at him that he couldn't hear. It was only when a bullet ricocheted off the gun barrel that Luke figured out what she must be saying. He vaulted over the sandbags and rolled away from the lagoon. He got to his feet and half ran, half slid down the hill toward the trees. When he reached them Sandy caught up with him and started beating on his back. He was thankful he couldn't hear any of the names she was calling him at that moment. He grabbed her hand and pulled her after him into the darkness.

It took nearly a half hour to find the ocean. They ran through the forest not worrying about the noise. It wouldn't have mattered if they had traveled slowly and quietly. Luke couldn't have heard any pursuit in his temporarily deafened state and there was no organized pursuit anyway. People were running around shooting at any shadow that moved, not sure who or how many were attacking them. When they finally reached the coast, Luke wasn't sure in which direction the boat was. He finally chose east and they crept along the shore. Sandy had given up trying to talk to him and settled for cursing under her breath. Finally they broke out onto a narrow beach and found their boat. It was a good thing they found it when they did because the wind had come up and waves were threatening to pull the boat out to sea.

In minutes they were out to sea and headed west around the island. It took nearly an hour to reach the beach on the southern shore of their smaller island. Wind and waves had slowed them and nearly made Sandy sick. When they pulled the boat up the beach and walked wearily back to the Waco it was nearly three o'clock in the morning.

Luke immediately dug around until he found a flashlight. With Sandy holding it he replaced the cut plug wire with one from the monoplane. That took a few minutes. When finished he motioned toward the plane and yelled, "Let's turn her around." Sandy shook her head and yelled back, "You don't have to shout!" With both of them pushing on one side of the tail they managed to shove it around until the nose of the aircraft was pointing toward the sea. When they had accomplished this they both leaned against the fuselage.

After catching his breath, Luke then attempted to start up the Waco. It took a bit but finally the engine fired into life. He listened to it for a minute then throttled back and got out. Taking the flashlight from Sandy he carefully looked over the running engine being careful to stay clear of the prop. From behind him she yelled, "What are you looking for?"

His hearing was returning slightly so he could barely hear her. Over his shoulder he shouted back, "You don't have to shout! I'm looking for oil leaks." Sandy threw up her hands in exasperation. Finding nothing, Luke shut the engine down. He looked at his watch and said loudly, "It's a couple hours 'til dawn. If they don't show up before then we might make it."

Sandy turned to him with a surprised look and shouted, "What? You don't want to stay and shoot up a few more of them? I'm shocked!"

Luke held up his hands in defense, "If we hadn't shot up that plane and the fishing boat they'd be all over us right now. This way, if we can get the Waco up we have a chance."

Sandy then inquired sweetly, "Ohhhh and you just shot up the submarine for fun?"

Luke shook his head rather guiltily, "No, that was personal. The Japanese have no business coming down here shooting up my neighborhood and making trouble. Besides, Roy was my friend. I was just paying them back a little."

Sandy thought about this for a moment, "Do you think you sank it?"

A shake of his head, "No, those things have reinforced pressure hulls." He said with a smile, "I sure didn't do it any good though." Sandy tried to look stern but eventually a smile slipped out, then a grin, and she burst out laughing. Luke joined in and they both laughed until they couldn't breathe. When she caught her breath she gasped out, "You were really something on that gun. Lying on the ground I could feel the concussion even with my ears covered." She touched him gently on the side of the head, "How's the hearing?"

"Coming back a little. It's going to be awhile though before it's right again."

He hesitated for a moment, "You did alright back there. Thanks for the help." Sandy blushed slightly. Luke smiled to himself as he picked up a machete. He gave another to her and said, "C'mon."

Picking up the axe he and Sandy set off across the field. They started chopping at any large bushes or small saplings Luke thought might mess up the Waco's take off roll. An hour later Luke was satisfied; the eastern sky was lightening and he judged they would soon have enough light for take-off.

They trudged back to the Waco and Luke gave it one more walk around after replacing the cowlings. There a few holes in the tail and a more in the wings but they were small and there were no rips. The control surfaces all moved easily. He decided they were as ready as they ever would be. He motioned Sandy toward the cabin when she stopped. He watched as she tilted her head. "I can hear them" she mouthed. Luke pushed her toward the cabin door, "Get in, now!" He jumped in as well and buckled his seat belt. Moments later he had the engine running. He turned to her and said loudly, "We don't have much room. I'm going to have to go out low to get my speed up." She nodded. He cranked down full flaps, shoved the throttle forward and yelled, "Hang on!"

The Waco rocked through the field gathering speed. It bumped along moving faster and faster. As they neared the narrow beach they had gained speed but not enough. They were moving slightly downhill and just as they neared the beach Luke caught sight of a large boat several hundred yards off shore directly in front of them. They flashed across the beach and Luke fought the urge to pull back on the stick. The wheels skimmed low above the water just clipping the wave tops as the speed built. Luke kept the nose down and prayed they didn't hit a high wave. The boat was ahead growing larger in the windscreen. Luke could see the damage to her superstructure. All the bridge windows had been shot out and there were holes and tears in the superstructure. He grinned. Out of the corner of his eye he could see Sandy white faced and gritting her teeth.

They flashed over the fishing boat no more than thirty feet in the air. The landing gear brushed across her masts and they were flying away low and fast. Luke gradually climbed upward. He looked at Sandy, who managed a weak grin, "Well, that was interesting." Luke smiled in return and turned north. As they neared the larger island he climbed to two thousand feet. He shouted at Sandy over the roar of the engine, "Let's take a look and see what's going on." They crossed over the lagoon from north to south. As they looked down Sandy was snapping pictures with her pocket camera. The lagoon was empty. The submarine was gone. They swept over the small hill and Luke could see the abandoned gun emplacement. There was practically no movement on the ground. They were over the airstrip in a second and there was plenty of movement there.

Sandy leaned forward to see what was happening. She could see small figures running around and then saw a large moving object. She gasped as she recognized an aircraft taxiing across the strip. She looked in amazement at Luke, "They got it running!" Luke nodded grimly. The Kawasaki had been repaired. The mechanics had probably worked all night. Above the engine noise he yelled, "If they get that thing up we've had it." Sandy said nothing.

Luke shook his head and pushed the stick forward. From two thousand feet they dropped like a stone. The airstrip was directly in front of them, the Kawasaki growing larger by the second. It was rolling fast down the strip. In seconds it would be airborne. Luke flattened his dive and came in low behind it. Cursing his lack of guns, he lined up above and behind the Kawasaki as it lifted off the ground. He could see the pilot glance over his shoulder as he skimmed across the tree tops. He was gaining speed and Luke's speed from the dive was bleeding off. He held his breath as they came in just a few feet above the Kawasaki.

As the two aircraft crossed the surf, Luke jerked the stick forward and then back. The Waco dropped four feet in the air and flattened out. Its wheels tore through the cloth and wood top wing of the Kawasaki with a ripping crash. Luke held the stick tightly and pulled up into a turn. Looking back, he saw the Kawasaki cartwheeling across the ocean.

Luke scanned his instruments as he put the Waco into a steady climb. Moving the stick gently he decided everything felt fine. He sighed in relief and plastered a cocky grin on his face, "Well I guess it's clear sailing now." Angrily Sandy punched him in the shoulder, "What the hell was that? You could have killed us!"

Luke replied weakly, "Well…it seemed like a good idea at the time."

Sandy shook her head, "Like I said; you need to work on your rescue technique."

Luke was fresh out of smart replies and concentrated instead on the oil pressure. Finally, Sandy spoke, "What do you think will happen now?"

Luke thought for a moment, "As soon as we make Miri I'll send a telegram to my boss telling him to alert the British and Dutch navies. They'll send somebody to check out that island." He shrugged, "They won't catch anybody but at least we've broken up their plan. Unfortunately, the Japanese are still out there making trouble and sooner or later there's going to be a war, I'm afraid."

Sandy just nodded, "Well, I've got a great story to tell. And I got out of there in one piece so I can't complain too loudly, but one thing…"Luke looked sideways at her, "What?"

She smiled and leaned back, "Next time could you ask your boss to send someone to rescue me who's not so crazy." Luke just shook his head and flew on.

The End

The Straits Agency Returns

So how did I come to write *Rescue*? Well, it's this way. Ever since I was a kid I've been in love with flying and aircraft. As a kid I built every German, British, Japanese and American aircraft model I could get my hands on. I even went out of my way to find obscure French and Italian aircraft to build. I also read every book on the air war during WWII I could find. Later on I went so far as to take flying lessons when I got out of the service. Flying has always been exciting and romantic to me. Looking back on all this it is not surprising that I decided to write a pulp air adventure. The surprising thing is why it took me so long to write one.

I have read a few of the air pulps like *G-8 and his Battle Aces* over the years. They were okay but I've always been more interested in the masked avenger type heroes so I never got too excited about air adventures. Then I ended up purchasing *The Blood and Thunder Guide to Pulp Fiction* a while back. This is a great pulp reference and through it I was exposed to many of the great pulp air stories and authors. I read some Philip Strange and Richard Knight adventures and liked them a lot. I also stumbled on the writings of Frederick Nebel. He wrote adventures of an imaginary flying detective company called *The Straits Agency* set in the South China Sea in the early 1930s. I found these stories lively and action filled and decided that I would be fun to revive some of Nebel's characters with some updated info and action. So I sat down to figure out a story line.

Nebel's stories took place in the early thirties. I decided that the very late thirties gave more room for action and intrigue. With a full scale war going on in China after the Japanese invasion in 1937 plus newer and updated aircraft and weapons, 1938-39 seemed a good time for adventures.

Choosing a plot wasn't a problem. For an air adventure all I wanted was a simple premise; a search for a downed reporter fit the bill nicely. All the rest was just writing the story. The hardest part, and the most fun, was researching all the aircraft and weapons. I spent a lot time digging into aircraft manufacturers in the 1930s and checking performance stats. So in the end, all that model building in my younger days paid off. I knew lots about aircraft and weapons of the time. In the end I think I got most of technical details right. As far as the actual writing, it went well and quickly. Action is something I'm comfortable with and I got to write a lot of action in this story. Although I didn't intend it I also ended up with a fun relationship between the lead characters; nothing too serious and certainly nothing that steals away from the action, but fun to write none the less. I think the whole story came out pretty well, hopefully readers will think so too.

Interestingly, when I came up with the idea for *Rescue* I had no place for it. I started it hoping I could eventually find a publisher. Then I had a talk with Ron Fortier at Windy City Pulp Con and pitched the idea for a new air anthology with lots of new characters from several time frames. He must have liked the idea because he eventually put out calls for *Aviation Aces*. By that time *Rescue* was already half written so it didn't take much to finish it and get it off to Ron. I'm really glad it found a home.

All in all, writing *Rescue* was a lot of fun. Now I'm not abandoning my love affair with the masked avengers to take up writing air stories but you never know; I might just try my hand at more of them down the road, especially now that we have this new air anthology. So keep your eyes open for more adventures of Luke Lance or some of the other interesting characters I've got my eye on. I hope you like *Rescue* as much as I do. See you next time.

✮ ✮ ✮

GENE MOYERS - studied European and Medieval history at the University of Oregon. He is a former U.S. Army armor crewman. He worked in the High Tech industry for some time and ran a store front and internet hobby shop for several years.

An avid military gamer and role player, his favorite game was *Daredevils* set in the 1930s. His love affair with the 1930s and pulps in particular stem from his first time reading a *Shadow* novel as a boy. Although interested in writing since a teen he did not turn to serious writing until 2000. He is the co-author of *GURPS Crusades* published by Steve Jackson Games. He has written stories for *Black Bat volume 3, Purple Scar volumes 1 &2, Domino Lady volumes 1 & 2 and The Phantom Detective volume 1*all for Airship 27. He has also written stories for Moonstone Books and Pro Se Press.

When not working on Airship 27 projects he is busy writing horror adventures for his swashbuckling character set in Colonial America and his new occult detective the Dream Master. Gene currently lives in Beaverton Oregon with his wife and two lazy dogs.

Windy City Widow

Andy Fix and Jeff Fournier

The cool air-conditioning washed over him as he entered the dimly-lit bar. Behind him, the door closed on the sweltering Midwestern summer afternoon. He hated traveling to these small towns in the middle of nowhere, but it was all part of the job description. He considered himself lucky if he could find an Applebee's or a BW3 on these business trips, but the best this town had to offer was a bar and grill named "Skip's."

As he looked around, he noticed the bar had an aviation theme going on. Dusty model airplanes hung on strings, old black and white photographs and WWII propaganda posters decorated the walls, and replica airplane noses hung from the rafters and spun propeller-shaped ceiling fans. Very quaint.

He sat down at the bar and stared at the bar-back. Instead of the typical mirror or shelves of bottles, a large, rust-covered metal panel hung on the wall. The original black color appeared faded from years of weathering, but he could still make out the image of a sultry pin-up girl and a name painted there.

"What is 'Windy City Widow'," he asked the man cleaning behind the bar.

"She was a P-61 Black Widow, like that one," replied the bartender as he pointed to one of the models hanging from the ceiling. "My grandfather flew her during WWII."

The model reproduced in miniature a rather odd looking plane. A turreted fuselage sat between two mid-level wings, and each wing sprouted a long tail boom. An engine nacelle connected each boom to the wing, and a single elevator spanned the two tail fins. The fuselage's long nose balanced out its fat rear end. The flat black paint scheme matched what he imagined the panel on the wall behind the bar would have looked like decades ago.

"A P-61?" He waved his hand dismissively. "Never heard of it."

The bartender chuckled. "Nah, and you probably never will. The Widows were night fighters; they flew in the darkness and shot down bad guys far from the spotlight the Mustangs and Warhawks and others got."

The man ordered a shot and opened up a menu. He looked back up at the panel and asked, "So, why is it you have a chunk of your grandpa's old plane hanging in your bar?"

The bartender placed the man's drink in front of him and smiled. "It's an interesting story, if you want to hear it."

The man looked at his watch and shrugged. "Sure, why not. Probably the most entertainment this town has to offer anyway."

The bartender leaned on the bar and looked back over his shoulder at the nose panel. "It all started back in England, 1944..."

✩ ✩ ✩

The inky black sea below him blended seamlessly into the moonless midnight sky. Without the instruments in front of him to tell him where the horizon separated the water from the clouds, Lt. Avery 'Skip' Colchord doubted he could keep this beast level. Skip had flown the air race circuit back in the States before the war, so he had no fear of dangerous flying. But skulking around in the dark and relying on instructions from his Radar Observer to tell him where to go hardly felt like flying.

Not that he would be doing any acrobatics anytime soon. The P part of the P-61's designation stood for 'Pursuit', as in 'Pursuit Fighter'. What a joke! The big twin-engine plane dwarfed other fighters. It probably could have been given a B designation and no one would have batted an eye. It sure flew like a bomber.

"Spinach Eater," said Skip into his throat microphone.

"What?" His R/O sat in a compartment in the rear of the fuselage, separated from the pilot by the empty gunner station and the yet-to-be-installed upper turret, so the two could only communicate through the intercom.

"We could name it 'Spinach Eater'; Moss could paint Popeye on the nose. You know, from the funny pages."

"Damnit, Skip, would you focus?" The pilot could hear the exasperation in his R/O's voice. "We've got to find this bogey before it reaches the coastline."

"Bluto Buster?" Colchord enjoyed annoying the man.

"I swear to God, I'm asking the Colonel to reassign me to another pilot when we get back. Now, keep scanning the sky for that contact."

"I am scanning, Pete." He still couldn't see anything but blackness outside of his cockpit windows.

A sudden flash of flame caught his eye. "Belay that. Tally-ho! Bogey at three o'clock, about a quarter mile away and about three thousand feet below. Looks like the exhaust plume from a buzz bomb."

"That's our contact, all right. Let's go get him, Skip."

Colchord banked the plane's wings and increased the power to the two massive Pratt & Whitney engines. The P-61 couldn't quite match the top speed of the jet-powered V-1, but the pilotless 'divers' were usually weighted down with enough explosives that they rarely came in at max speed. With his engines opened up full, he quickly closed with the flying bomb.

"Ease up on the throttle, Skip, you're closing too fast."

"Tell you what, Pete, why don't you let the actual pilot do the flying?" As he closed, Colchord lined the target up in his gun sights. The P-61 may not be a dogfighter, but it carried some heavy artillery. Even without the four .50 caliber machine guns that the missing turret would have contained, the Widow still carried four massive 20 mm cannons nestled in its belly. Since the engines were mounted in wing nacelles away from the plane's fuselage, the cannons lined up with the pilot's direct line of sight in front of him. But Colchord wanted to get as close as possible before taking his shot.

At five hundred feet the exhaust plume filled the gun sight like a blazing sun. Skip squeezed the trigger on his control stick, and a glowing line of tracer shells streaked towards the 'diver'. He twitched the yoke to the right after pulling the trigger, unwittingly saving his own life. The shells missed the jet engine at the rear of the V-1 and instead hit the bomb's warhead and ignited its 1,800 lbs of high explosives. The massive fireball blinded the pilot, but the belly of the plane took the brunt of the impact. Had Skip not veered off at the last moment, the cockpit would have been destroyed. He flew through the fireball with all of his limbs still attached.

Colchord blinked for several seconds before his vision cleared, and it took a few more before the instrument panel in front of him came into focus. Realizing the plane was in a steep dive, Skip pulled the control yoke back hard into his belly. After fighting the controls for what felt like an eternity, he managed to level the plane out just one hundred feet above the surface of the North Sea. With his ears still ringing from the explosion, he keyed his throat mic. "Pete, you okay back there?"

Nothing but static. Either the intercom was dead, or Pete was.

The plane responded sluggishly, and Colchord fought just to keep her level.

Looking out the left side of the cockpit, he saw why: the left wing looked like Swiss cheese, and his left engine blazed with fire. The mirror on the side of the cockpit showed a singed stump of metal where his left rudder should have been, and what remained of the tail elevator bounced jauntily in the slipstream. The rear fuselage trailed a plume of smoke, but he couldn't see enough to assess what damage the R/O compartment might have sustained.

"Hang on, Pete," said Skip into the intercom, hoping his R/O could hear him. "I'll get us home, I promise."

✪ ✪ ✪

"He called me a Mick! That galoot had it coming," Pvt. Mickey O'Brien said as his face reddened. He finished moving another can of ammo to the back of the jeep's trailer. His grousing about the confrontation with a British soldier last night at the pub in the nearby town of Ford started as soon as he rolled out of his bunk.

"But, Mick, that's what we call you," said Sgt. Glen Moss to the perturbed young ordinance loader. "And you don't try to deck any of us."

"But you guys don't mean it as an insult, Sarge. That Tommy wanted to pick a fight with me just for being Irish, so I obliged him!"

Moss slung his arm around Mick's shoulders. "Well, you can give him hell in the ring tonight, slugger. Both COs have approved the 'friendly' boxing match I suggested. Yah know, 'To ease the tensions between the units that share this town.'"

Mick's reply was cut off by the low drone of a plane engine overhead.

"Sounds like we got one coming back home," he said instead.

"And it doesn't sound good," replied Moss as he scanned the lightening dawn sky for the wounded plane. "There." The sergeant pointed to a slow moving silhouette of a P-61 that glowed in spots and trailed smoke. "Oh hell, she's on fire!"

As the plane approached the field, Moss wondered aloud at the extent of the damage. "Jeez-us! How is that thing even still in the air? That left wing is missing half of the control surfaces, and the left tail is completely gone. Who's flying that plane?" Moss stared in horror at the back end of the fuselage. The plexiglass tail-cone was gone entirely, and smoke billowed out of what remained of the R/O compartment. "That doesn't look good at all."

The plane faltered as the pilot fought to keep the wings level, but Moss saw that was the least of his worries. As the landing gear lowered, the situation went from bad to worse. Only the right landing strut deployed properly. The fire in the left wing's engine nacelle had destroyed the landing gear housed there, and the gear door in the nose only opened partially before jamming.

"He can't land like that, Sarge, he..."

"Clear out! Now," yelled Moss as he shoved Mick hard in the back.

The Widow's right wing dipped precipitously as the plane bled airspeed. The pilot somehow leveled out the wings again, but not soon enough. The plane stalled and plummeted to the ground. The right landing gear struck hard and the strut snapped off completely. The massive fighter impacted the ground belly first, rebounded twenty feet into the air, and then slammed back into the tarmac and careened directly towards them. As the plane slid towards them, the ammunition in its belly ignited, and 20 mm shells whizzed through the air where Moss and his crew had just been working.

Moss looked back over his shoulder as he and his men raced for cover. He saw several stray shells strike the A-20 Havoc they had just been loading for a photo recon mission. With a clap of thunder that assaulted his eardrums, the freshly fueled and armed plane exploded into a massive fireball. Flaming debris rained down around their position, but his crew had made it to the safety of cover.

Moss and his crew watched helplessly as the P-61 continued its slide right into the burning wreckage. The fire crews raced down the runway towards them, but the Widow was already engulfed in flames. They could see the pilot struggling to kick his way out of the cockpit, and the firefighters would never make it in time. Moss leaped to his feet, but Mick was already sprinting to the plane ahead of him.

"Mick! Get back here! That thing could go up any moment!"

Ignoring his own warning, Moss was just two steps behind the Private. Together they climbed the side of the plane and pried at the jammed hatch. The hot metal scalded their bare hands, but they weren't about to let that pilot cook inside. Mick's wiry muscles bulged as he pulled at the hatch, and Moss hammered the latch with a wrench he had in his pocket. Finally, the cockpit flew open and the pilot scrambled out into Moss' arms. The three of them fell to the ground in a heap as the fire crews screeched to a stop near the burning wreckage.

"Lt. Colchord," said Moss as he helped the officer to his feet. "Are you okay?"

"Grab Pete," wheezed the soot covered pilot between coughs.

They stumbled around to the back of the fuselage, only to find the R/O compartment a smoldering ruin.

Colchord stared in dismay at the empty operator's seat. "Oh, crap..."

✩ ✩ ✩

Skip Colchord stood at sharp attention in front of his commanding officer's desk. Though a slight man, Colonel Lionel Pollard still managed to cut an intimidating figure when his temper was up. He earned the nickname 'the Lion' for a reason.

"I should be congratulating you, Lieutenant," said the man seated behind the desk. "You just recorded the first 'kill' for the 422nd." He stood up and walked around the desk to glare at Skip's profile. His thinning gray hair told his age, but Pollard was still as fit as a fiddle. Colchord's own hair still held its full brown color, and he had at least four inches and a good forty pounds on the older man, but he was sure the Lion would have no trouble mopping the floor with him.

"Uh, thank you? Sir."

"Can it, Colchord," roared the Lion. "You're not getting off that easy for this! You may have downed that 'diver', but you also cost me two planes."

Skip straightened his stance even more and stared straight ahead out the window. "Yes, sir!"

"And consider yourself lucky that Lt. Stafford was fished out of the North Sea in one piece.

Skip tried to hide his sigh of relief. "So Pete's OK?"

"He's a bit singed, but he'll survive. He bailed out when the tail-cone was blown off."

"He should have had more faith in my abilities," said Colchord.

"You think you're hot shit, don't you, boy," snapped the Lion. "You flew in air races back in the States. Well, whoop-dee-doo. I cut my teeth shooting down Krauts over France the last time they held this dance. You're nothing special here, son."

"Permission to speak freely, sir," Skip requested.

"You always do anyway."

"I just think my skills are wasted flying a P-61, sir. I'm a fighter pilot, not a bomber pilot; I should be flying a P-51 or a P-47. Sir."

Pollard sighed and walked back around to the desk to his seat. "You're probably right, Colchord."

"Thank you, sir," said Skip as he relaxed and let a smile spread across his face. Finally! "If you could just put in a transfer..."

"Stuff it, hotshot!" The Lion shot to back his feet and pounded on his desk. "You're not going anywhere. Uncle Sam decides where your skills are best used, and right now that's right here in the 422nd Night Fighter Squadron. And until such time when Uncle Sam decides otherwise, you will put forth your best effort to do the job you're given, and to do it without killing any of my officers, ground crew, or airplanes! Do I make myself clear?"

Colchord snapped back to attention. "Yes, sir!"

"Now get the hell out of my office before I bust you down to mail plane duty."

☆ ☆ ☆

Skip walked out of the Nissen hut that served as the base's command center with his hands in his pocket and his head down. He stopped briefly when a flatbed truck carrying the twisted carcass of his plane rolled past. That did little to improve his spirits. He scuffed the dirt with his foot and continued on his way to the barracks. He didn't stop at the officers' rec hut as he strolled past it; socializing with others tonight didn't exactly appeal to him right now. He was so lost in his thoughts that Skip didn't even notice the jeep approaching until it pulled up beside him.

"Lt. Colchord," called out Sgt. Moss from the front passenger seat. "Are you coming into town tonight? Mick here is going to defend America's honor in a boxing match."

"It's going to be just like the fly-off next week, sir," said Mick with a grin on his face. "Just like our P-61 taking on the Brit's Mosquito. I'm going to box the ears off of that Tommy!"

Skip smiled at that. The bulky P-61 had about as much chance of outflying the Mossie as this kid did against the British paratrooper he had picked a fight with. The Widow so far failed to live up to expectations, and the brass wanted to ditch it in favor of the older but battle-proven British plane. Skip held out little hope for it winning the fly-off. Poor Mick, though, was going to get pummeled.

"Nah, you guys go on ahead without me. I'm still a bit shook up from my bumpy landing this morning."

The enlisted men all chuckled politely at Skip's attempt at levity. "Don't feel too bad about it, Lieutenant," said Moss. "I saw the condition that plane of yours. Took a lot of skill to fly that thing all the way back home. It was the plane that failed you in the end, not your piloting."

"That's nice of you to say, Sarge." Colchord waved farewell to the crew in the jeep and started to leave. He stopped when a second jeep, this one filled with several attractive Women's Auxiliary Corps servicewomen, pulled up.

"Can you tell us the way to town," asked the particularly pretty driver. She wore the wings of the Women's Airforce Service Pilots on her lapel. Interesting.

"Sure thing," replied Sgt. Moss. "You can follow us in."

The jeep started to pull away when Skip called out, "Hey Sarge, hold up a minute. I think I'll join you after all." He hopped up into the already crowded jeep and flashed the ladies his brightest smile. Today was looking to end a whole lot better than it had started.

☆ ☆ ☆

The pub in town overflowed with patrons as the crowd of regulars swelled with curious spectators. The pub owner had managed to squeeze a boxing ring into the middle of the floor, but that left little room for chairs. The cramped quarters meant that everyone stood elbow to elbow.

Skip Colchord leaned against the bar and watched as both fighters made their entrance. The big para towered over Mick, and his frame carried a hefty amount of muscle. Mick was thinner and shorter, but his wiry frame didn't have an ounce of fat on it. He looked like he could hold his own in most fights, just not against someone like his opponent tonight. Poor Mick.

Skip smiled broadly when he noticed the WASP from earlier making her way towards the bar. Her uniform cap sat daintily on top of her naturally curly shoulder-length brown hair, and the rest of her uniform couldn't hide the curves of her body no matter how hard its conservative military styling tried to. Yet despite this overwhelming femininity, she wore a look of competent seriousness on her perfect face. He aimed to turn those beautiful, stern lips into a smile by the end of the night.

She turned her head towards the ring as each fighter was introduced to a mix of boos and cheers. When she reached the bar, Skip extended his hand in greeting. "Hey there, Skip Colchord."

"A pleasure, Lieutenant," she replied as she shook his hand. "I'm Suzie."

The opening bell rang, and the two men in the ring circled each other slowly. Each fighter threw some quick jabs as they probed the other's defenses. The Brit towered over Mick, and the crowd clearly favored their countryman. Skip overheard even some Americans placing bets on the big para. He put a five spot on Mick, but only because he felt it was the patriotic thing to do.

"So what brings you over to this side of the pond, Suzie," he asked. "Other than those beautiful wings of yours, I mean."

"Oh, that was very smooth, Lt. Colchord. Do you use that on all the ladies?"

The crowd cheered as the Brit landed a series of solid punches to Mick's midsection. To his credit, the wiry redheaded American absorbed the punches and danced away from his opponent. He managed to keep the big guy at arm's length with a couple quick jabs of his own.

"Actually, that was my first attempt," said Skip. "I don't run into too many lady pilots over here."

"I see," she said with a cool smile. "If you must know, we ferried a handful of new B-24s over from the States to the 93rd stationed at Hardwick last week. And I flew an A-20 from there to here just a couple days ago. A recon upgrade."

Skip winced a little. "I, uh, I think ran across that earlier today."

Mick continued to dance around his opponent in the ring. The Brit threw more punches, but he missed more than he hit. Mick's own jabs weren't having much effect on the big guy, but the para was starting to tire noticeably. When the bell ending the round sounded, the Brit sat heavily onto the stool in his corner. Mick looked fresh as a daisy still, and he waved the offered stool away when he got to his side of the ring.

Suzie caught the bartender's attention and ordered a beer for herself. "I see you're a pilot as well, Lieutenant. What sort of plane do you fly? I imagine it's something sleek and fast like a Mustang."

"Er, no, there're no P-51s based here."

Mick came out of his corner at the bell and headed straight for his foe. He opened up his offense right away, taking some chances with heavier punches in between his jabs. The big Brit didn't seem to be hurt by any one of Mick's punches, but the cumulative effect was starting to wear him down.

"I see," said Suzie. "Then you must pilot one of those tough, rugged Thunderbolts."

"Um, nope. There're some P-47s stationed at the next airbase over, but none here at Ford." Skip took a big drink from his beer in an attempt to hide his discomfort.

"Well, whatever do you fly then, Lieutenant?"

The crowd around them cheered loudly. Mick clearly controlled the fight in the ring, now. He easily danced out of harm's way whenever the Brit took a swing, and each punch Mick landed now had an immediate effect on his opponent.

"I see you're a pilot as well, Lieutenant."

"I fly a P-61 Black Widow," Skip answered.

"Oh, a night fighter."

"You've heard of it?" Skip's face brightened with hope.

Mick landed a combo of quick punches to the para's body and face. The big guy didn't know where the next punch was coming from, and by the time he got a glove up to block; Mick was already pounding him somewhere else.

"Yes, I know what a P-61 is, Lieutenant." Her smile vanished. "Some jackass just flew one into the Havoc I brought in the other day."

With a heavy uppercut to the chin, Mick knocked his opponent to the canvas. The groggy Brit was still struggling to regain his feet when the ref reached eight, but the bell marking the end of the round saved him from being counted out.

"I don't date pilots, Lt. Colchord," said Suzie after finishing the last of her beer. "And certainly not reckless ones. Good night." Leaving cash on the bar to cover her tab, she made her way through the crowd towards the exit.

"Wow, you just crashed and burned for the second time in, what, twenty-four hours?"

Colchord spun to face the source of this comment. "Don't start with me, Styles, I'm not in the mood."

"Hear that, boys," Lt. Alan Styles said to the handful of men around him. "Hotshot here is too good to chat with us after downing three planes in a single mission."

Skip felt his face redden as his temper started to rise.

"Three," asked one of Styles' entourage. "I thought he shot down just the one."

"Oh sure," replied Styles, "he got the 'diver', and then two more planes on the ground."

The group of airmen burst into laughter, and Styles leaned in close and said, "You're the joke they're laughing at, Colchord."

Skip heard the bell starting the next round ring, and he came out swinging. His punch caught the unprepared Styles square in the chin. The pilot fell back into his entourage, spilling several beers and a couple servicemen to the floor. In such tight quarters, that one violent act sent a ripple of aftershocks throughout the crowd. People were inadvertently jostled, beers were accidentally spilled, and tempers started to flare among the already rowdy mob. Harsh words were exchanged, and arguments quickly escalated to scuffles. The packed pub was a primed powder keg, and Skip had just struck a match. An all-out brawl exploded.

The two men in the ring soon noticed the activity around them. They stopped swinging at each other and tried to process what exactly was going on. The boxers stood together in the middle of the ring in stunned silence, arms at their sides, and looked out over the sea of violence roiling around them.

☆ ☆ ☆

The Lion stared at Colchord from behind his desk, his anger a barely controlled volcano moments away from eruption. Skip particularly liked that comparison because Pollard's face turned a shade of bright red when he got this riled up. He could just picture the top of the colonel's head blowing off and red hot lava come shooting out.

"Colchord, you seem to be visiting my office entirely too often of late," said the Lion in a calm voice that belied the obvious rage boiling just beneath the surface.

"I enjoy your company, sir."

That may have been too much. Skip flinched as Mount Pollard erupted. Momma Colchord tried to raise a good boy, but Skip grew up on the mean streets of Detroit and spent years in airplane hangars with barnstormers, air racers, and mechanics. He'd been exposed to pretty much every swear word ever uttered, and even some that were made up. None of that prepared him for the burning tirade that rained down on him now. Skip was sure that some of the language assaulting him would leave actual bruises. Not that he needed any more of those right now. His could barely see out of his swollen left eye, and his lower lip felt about twice as big as it should have been.

After a few minutes of this verbal onslaught, Pollard stopped to catch his breath. He sat back down in his chair and spun it around to face the window overlooking the airfield. The CO sat like this for what seemed like hours before he finally heaved a big sigh and turned back around. "Do you know why you frustrate me so much, Colchord?"

A hundred witty responses passed through Skip's head before he decided a straight answer was probably the best choice under these conditions. "No, sir, I do not."

"You're an arrogant, smartass jerk who thinks he's God's gift to airplanes," said Pollard. "Nobody wants to work with you. And what frustrates me the most is that you're probably as good a pilot as you think you are."

Skip wasn't sure if he should be flattered or offended.

"And now I've got to reward you with a job that not only best suits your abilities, but also feeds into your overinflated ego with the potential to show off and gain some glory for yourself."

Skip's heart started beating double time. "I accept, sir. Whatever it is, I can do it." He could barely contain his excitement.

Pollard's mouth stretched to form what Skip could only assume was a smile of some sort. "I'm not surprised. This is one carrot that you couldn't ignore. There's someone here from HQ who will take over from here. Your mission training starts as of right now. You will give Captain Stark your undivided attention and your best effort. No goofing around or acting up, understood?

"Absolutely, sir. And thank you for selecting me, sir."

"Oh, I didn't select you, Colchord. Captain Stark requested you by name. This is your moment to shine, Lieutenant; don't mess it up for yourself."

Skip's brain could hardly process all of this good news. He came in here expecting to be busted down to flying a troop transport, but here he is being offered this opportunity. "I won't let you down, sir."

Pollard pressed a button on his intercom. "Please send in Captain Stark."

Skip heard the door behind him open as somebody walked in and stood at his side.

The Lion stood up and motioned to the person next to Skip. "Lieutenant Colchord, please meet Captain Stark, your Commanding Officer for the duration of this mission."

Putting on his most professional smile, Skip turned and extended his hand in greeting. "A pleasure..." His voice caught in his throat and his eyes bugged wide. "Uh..."

"Captain Suzie Stark, Lieutenant," said the officer. "We should dispense with pleasantries and get started right away. We're on a very short time table."

Mouth still agape, he turned to look at Pollard's beaming face. The bastard could barely contain his satisfaction with Skip's reaction.

"Oh, crap..."

☆ ☆ ☆

Lieutenant Colchord felt sweat trickling down his brow as they marched through the warm July air down the flight line. He'd held his tongue ever since the meeting in Major Pollard's office, but enough was enough. Turning to the woman walking next to him, Skip asked, "Suzie, just what the hell is going on here?"

Suzie Stark stopped and crossed her arms as she turned to face him. "Lieutenant, you will refer to me as 'Captain', 'Captain Stark', or 'Ma'am'. We are not on a first name basis. We have a job to do, and this is strictly business. Understood?" Without waiting for a response, she turned and continued her march.

"Yes, Ma'am, Captain Stark, ma'am." Skip hurried to catch up.

At the end of the line, he was surprised to see a P-61 being prepped for flight. The Widows didn't normally take to the air during the day. The twin tail booms sported freshly painted vertical black and white 'invasion stripes' painted over the standard olive drab coloration.

"Wait, are we flying this thing into France?"

"Not today, hotshot," replied Suzie as she grabbed a flight jacket that rested on one of the maintenance carts. "Today we are going to teach you how to fly an airplane."

Colchord scoffed at that. "Lady…er, Ma'am, I've flown the fastest, most maneuverable planes ever built against some of the best pilots in the world. I'm not sure what it is you plan on teaching me."

"I know," replied Suzie as she donned the flight jacket and a leather flight helmet. "I've seen you fly Gee Bees and Bulldogs. I know you can fly the pants off of any pilot in your unit. But this isn't a Model Z racer. I flew as lead test pilot for Northrop during the development of the XP-61. I know this plane inside and out, and I can show you how to make her dance."

"This beast? This thing handles like a battleship, and…wait, you what?" Skip replayed what Suzie had just been saying and was sure that he missed something somewhere. "When the hell did you see me race?"

Suzie tossed Skip a flight jacket of his own. "Suit up, Lieutenant, we're going for a ride."

Colchord hastily donned his flight gear as he weaved his way between the ground crew making their final preparations to the plane. He climbed up the access ladder to the cockpit hatch, only to find Captain Stark already in the pilot's seat.

"You're back there," she said as she motioned with her thumb to the empty gunner's station behind the pilot's seat.

Skip climbed up into the back seat and sat in sullen silence as Suzie went through the pre-flight checklist. Once the ground crew was clear, she fired up both massive Pratt & Whitney turbo-supercharged engines. The 2,100 horsepower monsters roared to life and Skip felt that comfortable buzz that always came over him whenever he felt the thrum of an airplane engine.

Suzie taxied to the runway and set the brakes. She pushed the throttle to the full power and looked back up at Skip and grinned. "Hang on to your pants, flyboy."

She released the brakes and the plane jumped forward. Within seconds they hit one hundred miles per hour. Not even a quarter of the way down the runway, Suzie jerked back on the control yoke and the Widow responded by leaping into the air. Pushed back into his seat by the quick ascent, Colchord could only watch in amazement. He had never seen a fighter take off after such a short roll, much less a plane the size of a medium bomber.

With the nose pointed almost straight into the sky and the engines red-lined, Suzie took the plane up to twenty-thousand feet and leveled off.

"How...how did you do that?" Colchord would never have guessed that a 30,000 lb airplane could be launched into the sky as quickly as she just did with this P-61.

"You ain't seen nothing yet." Suzie scanned the sky around her for a moment before adding, "Watch this."

As she banked the plane, Skip spied what Suzie was aiming for. A flight of P-47 Thunderbolts flying back to their own base passed about two-thousand feet below them. Suzie pushed the nose down and dived towards them at full speed. Skip yelped in alarm as she feathered the left engine in mid-dive, but she continued towards the fighters as if nothing happened.

Now it was the fighter pilots' turn to watch in shock. Not only did they pass the Jugs, but Suzie was rolling the plane slowly around the dead engine the whole way. After passing the stunned flyboys, Suzie gave them a waggle of the Widow's wings before peeling away. Skip watched as, one after the other, the Jugs each waggled their wings in response as a unanimous show of respect.

He could see Suzie's smile reflected in the cockpit glass. Wow, so she did have a heart after all. His own smile quickly disappeared as she started making a series of turns into the dead engine. With each turn, the nose of the plane would push down in an attempt to regain airspeed. But the Widow recovered quickly every time, and Skip could only wonder in amazement at the stability of the plane.

At twelve-thousand feet, and with the left engine still feathered, Suzie pulled back on the yoke and pointed the nose straight up again. Once they reached fifteen-thousand feet, she pulled back again, looping the nose over. As she rolled the plane over into an Immleman, Skip noticed the second engine feathering. "Uh, Suzie..."

"No need to worry, Skip, this is all part of the ride." Did he hear a note of warmth in her voice? Well, she wasn't insulting him, anyway, so that was progress.

Suzie executed a series of sharp turns and rolls as she guided the 30,000 lb glider back to the airfield. With a grace that belied its size, the Widow responded without complaint. Skip could only shake his head and grin along with Suzie. Between the plane's unexpected agility and the pilot's unexpected skill, Skip didn't know what he was more impressed with.

Skip took advantage of the silence to chat her up. "Where did you ever learn to fly like this?"

"Back home in Chicago." Suzie was silent for a moment. "My husband taught me."

Husband? Well, that explained everything! Relief flooded over him as he now understood why Suzie had rebuffed him at the bar. He wasn't losing his touch with the ladies, after all. "He must be some pilot, huh?"

Again, Suzie hesitated before answering. "He was the best, Skip. You should know; he was about the only pilot better than you."

Colchord sat in stunned silence for a moment. "Stark? As in Malcom Stark?" He tried frantically to gather his thoughts. "Oh crap, that would make you Mal's..." He couldn't finish as his mind replayed that horrible day in Oshkosh years ago. Mal Stark was indeed a hell of a pilot, right to the very end. One of the other planes clipped Mal's wing and sent him careening towards the stands. Mal avoided the spectators, but at the cost of his own life. He dove his plane nose first into the ground rather than crash into the grandstand.

"Mal's widow," Suzie finished for him.

Sgt. Moss wiped the sweat from his brow. He looked over his shoulder for his help, only to find Pvt. Mickey O'Brien staring off into the sky while shielding his eyes from the bright afternoon sun with his hand.

"Do you hear anything, Sarge?" Mick still stared off into the distance.

Moss looked over at Mick in silence for a moment and wondered if he should smack him upside the head or not. "Nothing but me and the rest of the crew working. Why?"

"That plane overhead, Sarge." Mick pointed to a plane slowly circling the airfield as it dropped in altitude. "Shouldn't it be making some noise? Like, engine noise?"

Moss walked over to see what Mick was looking at. He assumed that the kid had taken one too many shots to the head in the ring last night. After briefly scanning the sky, the sergeant saw what his ordinance handler was talking about. "What the hell?"

They watched the P-61 line up for an approach to the runway. Sure enough, it wasn't making a sound. Both props were feathered. Moss could only shake his head. "What is it with these crazy landings this week?"

The plane was coming in smooth and level, if a bit fast. The gear dropped as the Widow made her final approach, and the pilot gracefully set the plane down first on its wing mounted wheels, and then on the nose wheel. The screeching of the tires as they touched the runway sounded oddly loud without the roar of the engines to deafen everyone. The pilot deftly applied the brakes and slowed the speeding plane down. After short roll down the runway to bleed off more ground speed, the Widow made a sharp ninety degree turn and came to a smart stop just a few feet away from them. Moss couldn't help but be impressed.

A moment later, the canopy hatch popped open and a grim looking Suzie Stark climbed out. The instant her feet hit the pavement she marched off without saying a word. An ashen-faced Skip Colchord climbed out of the gunner's station and dropped to the ground right behind the pilot. He doffed his flight helmet and stood staring after her while scratching his head. Moss came over to check on him.

"You run into some turbulence up there or something, Lieutenant?"

"Yeah," replied Skip, clearly distracted, "something like that."

Colchord glanced at his instrument panel to confirm his altitude. He brought them back up to twenty-thousand feet and leveled his wings. Everything went smooth as silk.

"All right, Lieutenant, let's try this again," came a voice from the gunner's station behind him. "You're still holding back."

"Ma'am, I don't want to crash this thing," Colchord replied. "I'm pushing her as far as she can go." Twice he had run through Suzie's instructions, and both times he aborted halfway through. The plane just wasn't built for this type of flying. It kept wanting to stall on him, which would lead to a nosedive into the deck.

"You need to get past your preconceptions of what this plane can and cannot do, Lieutenant," came Suzie's stern reply. Ever since their little chat towards the end of yesterday's flight, she'd given him the cold shoulder. The sub-zero temperatures of the atmosphere outside the plane seemed more welcoming than being inside this cockpit.

"I'm sorry about Mal, Suzie. And I'm sorry I missed the connection between you two."

"Lieutenant Colchord," she snapped back, "you need to focus on the mission at hand. Today is July 2, and the competition against the Mosquito is July 4. We have less than forty-eight hours to get you up to speed."

"Yes, ma'am." Skip banked the P-61 and brought it around for another run. "But why me, Captain? You clearly don't like me, and you've shown that you can make this plane do the impossible."

"Okay, Skip, I'll level with you, but only if you promise to let loose and fly this plane like I you're told."

Did he notice a slight thaw in the chill? "You have a deal, Captain."

"First, I'm not flying in the competition because the brass insisted that the pilot of each plane be an active duty service pilot from the USAAF and the RAF. No ringers. I'm a qualified pilot, and I was part of the flight testing of the XP-61 for Northrop during the Widow's development. But my WASP wings aren't considered USAAF wings, and my officer's status isn't a US Army commission. I can beat any RAF pilot they put up in the Mossie, but they won't let me."

Skip couldn't argue with that. He experienced firsthand what Suzie could do with this plane, and he still struggled to wrap his brain around it. Hell, if he flew the Widow like that, they would win the fly-off hands down.

"Second, I picked you for this mission because of all the pilots in the 422nd Night Fighters Squadron, your unique set of piloting skills makes you the most qualified pilot available."

"Unique set of skills?" Colchord knew he was better than any other pilot in the 422nd, but what 'unique' skillset did he possess?

"I'm not supposed to divulge this information, but you'll be flying a timed flight through a closed course around a set of pylons." He could almost hear her smiling. "Skip, you'll be flying in an air race like the dozens you've flown before."

"Hundreds," he replied with a smile of his own. "Suzie, I do believe we've got a chance to win this thing." Skip had lined the nose of the Widow up with the imaginary course she'd been having him fly. He could practically see the pylons floating in mid-air now.

"Not until you fly this thing right, Skip. Now punch it!"

Colchord pushed the throttles all the way to the firewall, and the engines responded with a throaty roar. He banked to his wings ninety degrees and cut a sharp turn that pushed him against the opposite cockpit wall. The nose bucked and the plane stalled as the nose dipped. Skip instinctively went to throttle back and level it out, but Suzie's voice stopped him.

"Push through it, Skip! Don't let up. She won't hurt you."

This time Colchord did as she said. He ignored his instincts and kept the engines wide open as he stood the Widow on its wingtip. Sure enough, the nose dipped a bit, but he was able to maintain control. It was almost as if the plane was flying with him, not against him. She dipped her nose to pick up airspeed, but made it through the turn without losing control.

"See," said Suzie from behind him. "She's a fighter plane after all, isn't she? The Widow is the safest, most modern plane in the sky. She'll surprise you if you trust her."

The engines still screamed, and Skip moved to throttle them back a bit. The last thing he wanted to do is blow an engine in mid-flight.

"Hands off that throttle, Lieutenant," said Suzie, but her voice had lost the edge it had earlier. "These Pratt & Whitney engines are the best in the world. You can keep them at full power for as long as you like and they won't fail you. You're going to need all the speed you can muster when flying that course. The Widow will give you that speed. All you need to worry about is guiding her through the pylons. Trust her, Skip, and she'll stand by your side the whole way."

"Yes, ma'am," he replied as he pulled his hand away from the throttle.

"And, Skip," she almost whispered into the intercom, "I never said I didn't like you."

"What was that, Captain," he asked with a grin spreading across his face. "I didn't copy that last transmission."

"Shut up and fly, Lieutenant."

With his heart pounding and a smile on his face, Skip executed a series of high speed turns, rolls and loops that he thought impossible when he climbed into this cockpit this morning. His confidence grew with each maneuver, and he pushed the plane harder into every turn. The Widow responded flawlessly, matching his commands with agility that belied her size. This was the fighter plane he'd been wanting to fly! He let out a whoop of joy as he spun the plane into a continuous barrel roll over the airfield below.

"Mr. Colchord," said Suzie, giggling freely, "I think we're ready for that competition."

Skip executed…high speed…rolls…

Skip ran his hand down the leading edge of the P-61's wing as he approached the crew maintaining the starboard engine. The engine nacelle access panel hung open, so all he could see were two pairs of legs sprouting from beneath the cowling. Sergeant Moss, the head of this ground crew, stood next to whoever was under there handing them tools.

"Just tuning her up for tomorrow, Lieutenant," said Moss as Skip approached the crew. "Which reminds me, you still haven't given her a name yet, have you?"

Skip glanced up at the bare olive drab nose panel. Every other plane on the line sported at least a name painted there, and most were decorated with some pretty spectacular nose art. Sultry dames striking seductive poses with suggestive names were the popular choice, but cartoon characters or homages to hometowns cropped up on a few of the Widows. Save for a lonely looking V-1 silhouette kill marker, the nose of Skip's P-61 was a blank canvas.

"Still working on that one, Sarge. I'll let you know as soon as inspiration strikes. What'cha working on?"

Corporal Casey Cabrera poked his grease-smeared face from beneath the cowling. "Just a few tweaks, Sir," said the mechanic with a mischievous grin on his face. "We want her to be at her best, right?"

This gave Skip pause. Cabrera's reputation as a gambler was notorious on base. He himself had been fleeced more than once in a card game by the affable Californian, and he'd learned to avoid getting suckered in when Cabrera pulled out his ever-present deck of playing cards. Rumor had it that he wasn't afraid to 'tweak' things in his favor.

"Um… Casey, are you sure that's wise?" Casey's skill as a mechanic surpassed his even impressive skill as a gambler, but any 'tweaking' might compromise the integrity of the engines. The last thing he wanted was for an engine to fail spectacularly during the fly-off. "Where exactly did you get the idea for these adjustments?"

"He got them from me," came a feminine voice from inside the engine cowling. Suzie Stark peeked at him around the open access panel. He almost didn't recognize her with her face covered with even more grease than what Cabrera wore. "Trust me on this, Skip, I know what I'm doing."

"Oh, c'mon, Suzie, you're an airplane mechanic now, too?"

"I was Mal Stark's chief engineer before I became his wife, Lieutenant," Suzie responded with a bit of fire lighting her eyes. "And if I recall correctly, his planes were faster than yours on a regular basis. And like I told you earlier, I know the P-61 inside and out, every bit of it."

Skip held up his hands in deferment. "Hey, I've learned my lesson. I trust you guys. But is it legal under the terms of this competition?"

"They said no non-service pilots are allowed to compete," said Suzie with a twinkle in her eye. "They never said anything about non-service mechanics." With a wink, Suzie ducked back under the cowling and continued with her work.

"All right, have at it. Just know that I'll be pissed if you guys get me killed."

Skip instantly regretted these words as Suzie ducked her head back down to glare at him. She showed no signs of the playfulness from just a few moments ago.

"Ah, sorry," Skip stammered. "I'll be leaving now." He turned and headed back towards the Nissen hut that held the officers rec room. Moss heard him cursing himself under his breath as he walked by.

✩ ✩ ✩

The temperature rose steadily as the sun cooked off the morning fog that covered the airfield. Though he couldn't see them, Colchord could hear the ground crews working the winches as they raised several barrage balloons into the sky. The makeshift pylons formed the course that he and the Mossie pilot would navigate in their competition in a couple hours. Both planes were already lined up on the tarmac as their crews worked through the pre-flight check lists and made final adjustments.

"Lieutenant Colchord," called a man in uniform as he approached him with his hand extended. "Captain Drummond, RAF. Good day for a hop in the sky, what?" Skip could swear the man's perfect teeth twinkled as he smiled at him.

"Yes, sir, it sure is." He took the man's offered hand and shook it firmly. "Can I say that it's quite an honor to compete against you, Captain?"

"No need for formalities, chap. Call me 'Bulldog'. Everyone else does, whether I like it or not," he said with a wink.

Skip guessed that Drummond was quite fond of the nickname. He had to admit that the Brit earned his reputation for being a tenacious fighter. The man's Mosquito parked next to his own Black Widow sported several swastikas next to the cartoon bulldog painted on its nose. And the train silhouettes painted below those aerial kill markings indicated that the British Bulldog wasn't afraid to get down and dirty on ground attack missions. And was that a U-boat painted on there, too? Impressive resume.

Up until a few days ago, Colchord would have never dreamt of taking a P-61 on an attack mission, but he thought differently now. Bring on the bad guys!

"Best of luck to you, Bulldog. I think you might need all you can get today," said Skip with a wink of his own.

The Brit laughed affably and patted Colchord on the shoulder. "Cheerio, Yank! May the best plane win." With a wave, Captain Drummond turned and headed over to his plane to assist the ground crew with their preparations.

Skip walked over to his own plane and went over final instructions with his team. Suzie Stark and Casey Cabrera explained the modifications they made to the engines, and Moss went over the pre-flight with him. By 0900, the fog had lifted, and for the first time Skip could see the barrage balloon pylons that marked out the course. He'd flown tighter courses as an air race pilot back in the States, but those were in highly maneuverable stunt planes. Even with his new-found appreciation for the Widow's capabilities, this course looked challenging.

The British Bulldog drew the short straw, so he took his Mossie through the course first. The man certainly could fly, Colchord would give him that. The twin-engine de Havilland Mosquito was crafted mostly of wood and fabric, and it weighed far less than the bulkier all-metal P-61. So even though its two Merlin engines didn't produce quite the horsepower the Widow's Pratt & Whitneys did, the sleeker, lighter British plane could match the P-61's top speed.

Capt. Drummond navigated the course expertly. He didn't miss any of the turns, and he kept up an impressive speed as he weaved through the pylons. As he came out of the final turn, he lined up the brightly painted target balloon in his sights and opened up with all four of his 20 mm cannon and his four Browning 7.7 mm machine guns. The hydrogen-filled balloon went up in an impressive fireball as all of the Mossie's shells struck home.

After the British contestant landed and cleared the runway, Skip taxied his plane up to the start line. He stood on the brakes and pushed the throttles to full as he waited for the flagman to give him the signal to start. He took a quick glance over at spectators lining the runway and picked Suzie out of the crowd. He gave her a wave she probably couldn't see, but it heartened Skip to know she was watching.

Out of the corner of his eye he saw the flag drop. Focus, Skip! He released the brakes and the Widow took off down the runway like a rocket. An instant later, he pulled back on the control yoke and pointed the nose almost straight up. The P-61 responded perfectly, and he chewed up altitude at a blinding pace. At the designated altitude, Skip leveled off and circled around to line himself up with the course below. He pushed the nose over slightly and started his run.

As he approached the first barrage balloon, the English countryside disappeared and he was flying his Model Z race plane through the twisting pylons set up in Cleveland, or Chicago, or Oshkosh, or any of a dozen other air race courses. He focused only on the next pylon, the next turn, and then the turn after that. The g-forces pressing him back into his seat were a lover's embrace, quickening his heart and bringing sweat to his brow. He flew the course like it was the last race he would ever fly.

The brightly colored balloon racing towards him snapped him back to reality. At the last instant, Skip pressed the trigger on his yoke. A stream of 20 mm shells pierced the target balloon's fabric skin just before his plane did, and the ensuing fireball billowed all around him. "Oh, crap!"

Luckily for Skip, the hydrogen explosion was all flash. The fireball scorched some paint off his plane, but it lacked the explosive impact the V-1's warhead carried. After blinking away the tears caused by the balloon's blindingly bright demise, he reoriented himself and found the runway.

Fearing he lost precious seconds in the aftermath of the explosion, he made his final approach on the landing strip at full speed. This was going to be uncomfortable. He lowered his gear and brought the plane down hard on the runway. After rebounding once, all three wheels made contact with the ground. Skip stood on the brakes and rolled to a stop after just a thousand feet, hitting his mark exactly.

As he killed the engines, Skip rested his head on the control yoke. The adrenaline pumping through his veins washed over him, and it took him a moment to slow his racing heart. By the time the props stopped spinning, several of the US officers and servicemen were rushing towards the plane. He worried that he was still on fire, but then he saw the jubilant smiles on their faces and heard their cheers. With a sigh of relief, Skip popped the hatch and climbed out of the cockpit.

✩ ✩ ✩

Skip entered the officers club to a chorus of cheers. The sun hadn't even reached noon yet, but several bottles of champagne had already been popped open and alcohol was flowing freely. Benny Goodman's 'Sing, Sing, Sing!' played on the jukebox, and several officers were spinning with WACs on a makeshift dance floor.

"Good job today, Skip," said Colonel Pollard as he approached Cochord. "Though we could have done without the theatrics at the end." He wore that strange look on his face that Skip took to be his smile.

"Thank you, sir. That was entirely unintentional, I assure you."

"I'm sure it was," replied the Lion with a wink. "Whatever the case, you won the day. Your time beat the Brit's handily, and the brass has settled on the P-61 going forward. You've upheld the honor of the Black Widow, of the 422nd, and of the United States Army Air Force as a whole. Congratulations are certainly in order. Feel free to enjoy some champagne."

Skip took the proffered glass and moved on through the crowd. Suzie had to be around here somewhere. He stopped and turned when he heard a familiar voice snap, "Colchord!"

"Look, Styles, we're not doing that…" Skip stopped when he saw Lt. Styles' hand held out towards him and a genuine smile on the man's face.

"Don't worry, Skip, I'm not looking to start any trouble," said his nemesis. He grabbed Colchord's hand and pumped it several times in a vigorous handshake. "I owe you an apology. That was some flying you did today, chum."

"Yeah, thanks," Skip said to his newfound best 'friend'. "Hey, can we chat later? I have to hit the head." Skip was already scanning the crowd for Suzie. He felt a friendly clap on his back as he walked away. What a jerk.

Over in the corner, Colchord spied a group of familiar servicewomen seated around a table. As he made his way over, he saw Suzie Stark's beautiful face among them. He felt the corners of his mouth turn up into a giddy smile. Ease back on the throttle there, Skip. "Hello, ladies."

Suzie greeted him with a radiant smile. She wore her smart WASP uniform now, not the grease-covered mechanic's overalls she had on this morning before Skip's flight. He couldn't decide which look suited her better, but she looked drop dead gorgeous no matter what outfit she wore.

"Oh, Skip, you did it!" She flung her arms around his neck and hugged him warmly. Before he could help himself, he started picturing her in no outfit at all. With a deliberate effort, he stopped his brain from going down that road.

"Couldn't have done it without you, Captain Stark, ma'am," he replied, his own smile still lighting up his face. "Col. Pollard says a celebration is in order. You know of any going on?" Skip looked around the room as if it were empty.

Suzie giggled lightly. "I think we should skip the formalities, Lieutenant," she said with mock sternness. "We're on a very short time table."

Grabbing Suzie around the waist, Skip backed them onto the dance floor and started slowly turning her around in a lazy Lindy dance. Miller's 'In the Mood' played on the jukebox now, and it certainly set the proper mood.

"Time table," he asked her as they danced, "what time table is that?"

"Oh, Skip, I'm… I'm sorry. I thought you knew." All playfulness had left her eyes. "I'm leaving this afternoon. I'm flying back home to Chicago."

He stopped dead in his tracks in the middle of the dance floor. "You're what?" His stunned body refused to move, forcing the other dancers to twirl around them. "Suzie, you can't leave. We… we…"

"I have to, Skip," she said with tears brimming in her eyes. "My superiors already have new orders for me." She put her head against his shoulder and hugged him tightly. "I… I can't do this," she whispered. Without another word, Suzie Stark unwrapped her arms from around him and walked out of his life.

☆ ☆ ☆

Skip Colchord walked through the chill December air towards the flight line. Snow crunched beneath his feet and he looked out across the freshly plowed runway. Though most of the snow had been cleared off, taking off and landing on it in the dark of night was bound to be tricky. As one of the few Nazi airfields left relatively intact by the Allied advance through Belgium, Skip knew that even these difficult conditions were still better than some of the rougher fields other Allied pilots had to deal with across the Continent.

He arrived at his plane and whistled out loud in appreciation. Gone were the familiar olive drab paint scheme and the garish black-and-white invasion stripes he had gotten used to seeing on his plane. The P-61 in front of him now sported a sleek black overall paint job. The only color was in the brightly painted portrait and name decorating the nose.

"She looks fantastic, Sarge," he said.

Moss looked up from the ammo cart he was pushing over to the belly of the plane. "Thanks, Captain. With a subject like that, I had to do her justice. You made a good choice, sir."

Skip ran his hand down the script writing that spelled out 'Windy City Widow'. Leaning over the plane's name was a portrait of a sultry mob moll wearing high-heeled shoes, a skimpy pin-striped skirt, and a matching suit coat that hung open. And nothing else. In her hands she held a smoking Tommy gun. But her face is what Skip's eyes lingered on.

"The likeness is incredible, Sarge. You did that from memory?"

"Yes, sir," Moss replied as he and Mick started loading the 20 mm shells into the belly guns. "Captain Stark had a face that's hard to forget, sir."

"Tell me about it." He'd been trying to forget her for the better part of six months. "Mick, you suited up and ready to go?"

"Yes, sir. As soon as we get this magazine loaded, I'm good to go."

"All right. This is your first time up since we got the turret installed, isn't it?"

"Yes, sir, but I've done all the training, and I qualified ahead of all the other gunners."

"I wouldn't have expected anything less, Champ." Colchord looked up at the newly installed upper turret and the barrels of four fifty caliber machine guns sticking out from the front of it. A welcome addition to the plane's arsenal, as was the gunner himself, but the extra weight and drag that came with the package was still a question mark in Skip's book. He hoped it wouldn't slow him down.

Another officer fully suited up approached the plane. "Flight Officer Dakota Ralter reporting for duty, Captain," said the fresh-faced young man. He snapped off a smart salute in Skip's direction. "I'm your new R/O, sir."

"Very good, Ralter. Welcome to the team. You feel up to a little action?"

"Right now I feel I can take on the whole Reich by myself, sir."

"Let's just worry about the Krauts in the immediate vicinity tonight, son," said Skip with a smile. Yeah, he had to break in two new crew members on this flight, but he really couldn't hold that against either guy. Mick had been a member of his ground crew since the beginning, and just about every other flight crew had promoted their ammo loader to the gunner position once the new turrets were installed. As for the new Radar Operator, well, young Flt. Officer Ralter certainly couldn't be blamed for Pete Stafford being rotated back home to the States.

"Mount up, gentlemen," said Skip as he climbed up to the cockpit. "We've got some hunting to do tonight." He climbed up into the cockpit and strapped in. He heard Mick clamber up into the gunner's station behind him and close the canopy hatch. An intercom check confirmed that Ralter was secured in the R/O compartment in the back of the fuselage.

After running through the pre-flight checklist, Skip fired up both engines and taxied down to the end of the runway for take-off. After the tower gave him clearance, Skip throttled up and took to the air.

He hoped that tonight's hunt proved fruitful. The Allied fighters had wiped the daytime skies clean of any Luftwaffe planes, but the dark of night still harbored the enemy. The only German pilots left were either inexperienced rookies or hardened survivors. The latter piloted the Luftwaffe's deadly night fighters, and their bravery, ingenuity, and skill made them formidable

70   Andy Fix & Jeff Fournier

opponents indeed. Skip relished the thought of engaging an enemy ace in
a duel in the dark.

Several hours of empty flying droned by until Ground Control
Intercept piped up on the radio indicating a contact. "Copy that, GCI,"
Colchord transmitted into the radio. Thumbing the intercom button, he
said, "Hear that, Dak? Let's find out what Jerry's up to out there." They
circled in a search pattern for several minutes, but nothing appeared on
Ralter's scopes.

Noticing his low fuel level, Skip started turning for home when Mick
called out behind him.

"Over there, Skip! At three o'clock and down on the deck. Do you see it?"

He glanced in that direction, but he couldn't quite figure out exactly
what he was seeing. The plane's silhouette made it out to be a Ju 88, a
German twin-engine medium bomber and all-around utility player for
the Luftwaffe. It flew just under radar detection level, about five hundred
feet off the ground and at about two hundred mph, but what was confusing
was the fact that it dropped a line of flares at regular intervals as it moved
along a straight course. Why fly that low to avoid radar detection but then
lay out a trail of flares pointing right at your ass end?

"Well, hell, boys," said Skip as he shook his head, "Jerry's just begging
us to shoot him tonight." He circled around to line up behind the 88 when
he noticed something else odd.

"Mick, tell me what you see about two thousand feet behind our flare
farting friend down there."

After a brief pause, Mick answered. "Looks like another plane, Skip.
Twin tails, like ours."

Into the intercom, Colchord asked, "Dak, did we drift over into anybody else's patrol grounds?"

"Negative, sir," came the reply. "But that's not a P-61. It's too small.
Looks like a P-38 to me, sir."

"Good call, Dak. I think you're right." Skip knew that some night fighter
units in the Pacific had modified their P-38 Lightnings to hunt at night as
a stop-gap measure until the P-61's rolled out, but he'd never heard of any
NFS in the European theatre doing that. Curious, he dropped down to the
smaller plane's level and approached slowly to identify himself. The last
thing he needed was for a trigger happy day-timer getting spooked and
shooting up his plane.

He leveled off next to the P-38 and flashed his navigation lights. When
the other pilot looked over, Skip gave him a friendly salute.

"Um, Skip, there's something funny here."

"What is it, Mick?"

"Why is there a swastika on this guy's tail?"

"A what...?" Skip's inquiry was cut off as the P-38 banked suddenly into a high-speed turn away from them. "It's a trap," he yelled into the intercom as he broke in the opposite direction. "Dak, don't lose contact with that guy!"

Getting into a turning gunfight with the nimble Lightning held little appeal for Skip. How the hell did Jerry get his hands on a P-38, anyway? Their only advantage lay in the fact that they could see in the dark and their enemy couldn't.

A blinding beam of light washed over the 'Widow', followed quickly by a glowing stream of tracers. Okay, maybe Jerry wasn't so blind. This P-38 obviously carried some pretty powerful spotlights. If necessity was the mother of ingenuity, desperation was the father. "Damn, these guys are resourceful!"

Skip tipped the Widow on its left wingtip and cut a sharp turn. He knew he couldn't out-turn the Lightning, but he counted on the Nazi pilot knowing that, too. Sure enough, the German cut a tighter turn in an attempt to line up another shot. When he saw the beams from the spotlights pull slightly ahead of his nose, Skip yanked the control yoke the opposite direction and rolled over into a tight S turn. Before the enemy could find him with his high-beams again, Colchord went full throttle and pulled his nose straight up and over into a loop. While inverted, he peered out the top of his cockpit towards the ground and spotted the other plane's bright headlights searching for the P-61. "Gotcha," he said as he looped down behind his target.

The German pilot realized too late what had happened. The instant the Lightning was in range, Mick opened up with a broadside from the Widow's full arsenal. The enemy tried to evade, but several shells ripped into his right engine, shearing the wing off at the nacelle and setting the engine on fire. The rugged P-38 might have survived such a strike at a higher altitude, but this close to the ground gave even the most experienced pilot little time to react. The German lost control and the plane tumbled out of the sky; a trail of fire splattering across the ground marked its demise.

"Got him! I got him," yelled Mick.

"Great, kid! Don't get cocky," replied Skip. "Dak, where's that Eighty-Eight?"

"I'm looking now, no contacts."

The reason the enemy plane didn't appear on the R/O's scopes soon became evident. A blaze of tracer fire past his cockpit window and the sickening thuds of shells impacting metal told Skip exactly where the other German was. He jerked back on the yoke quickly, which kicked the P-61's

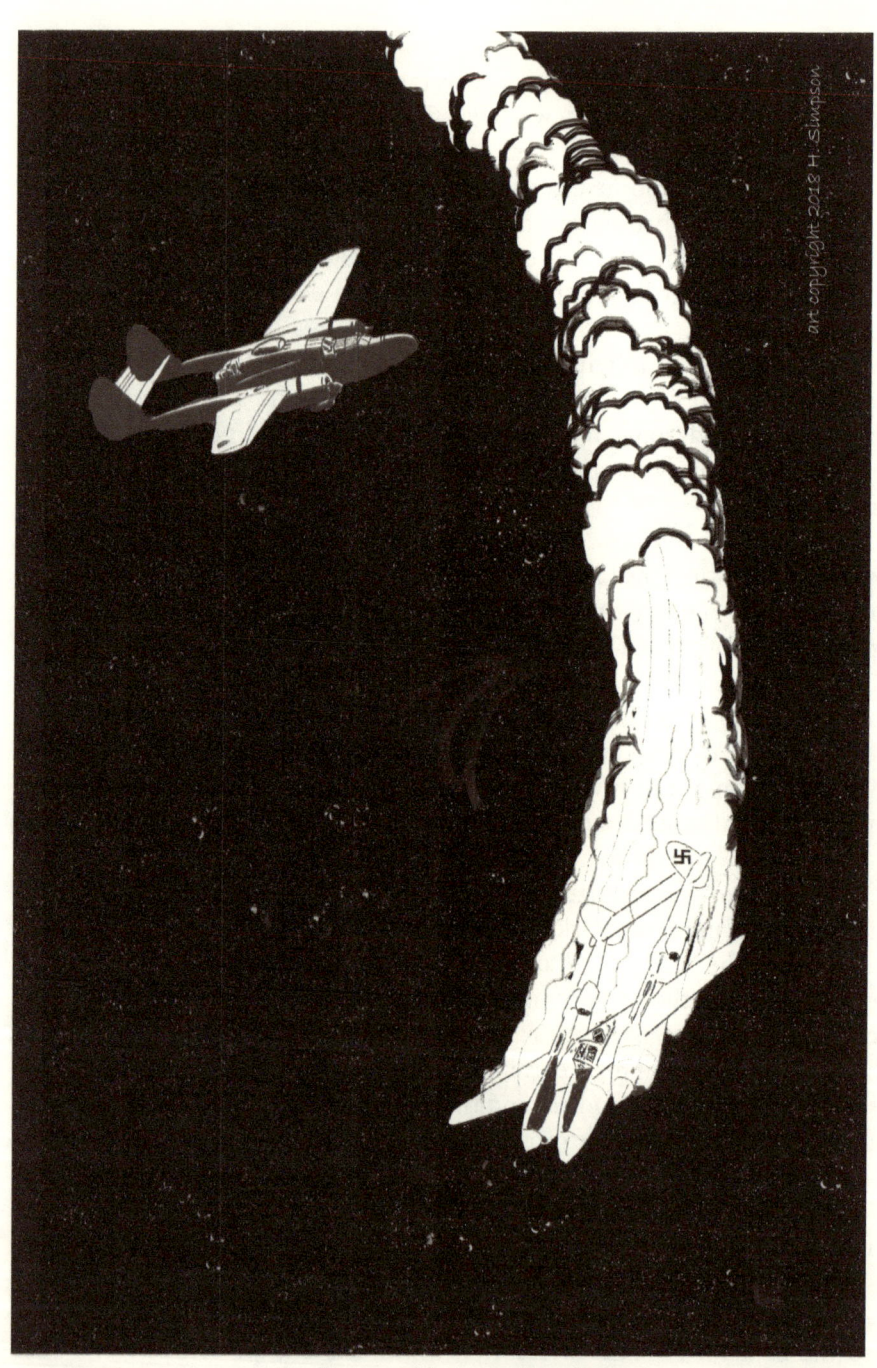

...the plane tumbled out of the sky...

nose up. The 'Widow' flared up, and with its now-vertical big wings acting as a massive airbrake, she shed airspeed instantly. The Eigthy-Eight zoomed past underneath, and before the German pilot could react, Skip pushed the nose back down and dove toward the enemy's top side. Without needing to be told, Mick triggered the four 20 mm cannons in the belly. The shells tore through the 88s fuselage and up into the cockpit. The bomber flew level for a moment, then it slowly keeled over to the side and fell into a dive. Skip circled around until a large explosion flashed from the ground below.

"I'm calling it a night, gentlemen. We're low on fuel. Dak, are the scopes clear? I don't want any more surprises popping up."

There was no response.

Pilot and gunner stood by silently as the medical crew removed Flt. Officer Ralter's body from the shattered R/O compartment. The Ju 88 hit them with a 20 mm cannon and a trio of 7.92 mm machine guns, and the young R/O took a cannon shell through his chest. He died instantly, of course, but that did little to salve his crewmates' grief.

"There's two less Krauts shooting up our guys now, Skip," said Sgt. Moss. "That's gotta be worth something."

"Yeah, I know, Sarge. Doesn't hurt any less, though. Damn, he was just a kid." Skip nodded towards a C-47 parked at the next hangar over. A ground crew scurried around it unloading several crates. "What's the skinny on that?"

"Landed about thirty minutes before you did," answered Moss. "Real hush-hush. Flight crew was whisked away in a jeep before I got here. I believe they're meeting in the Lion's Den as we speak."

"Well, hell. That can't be good."

No sooner had those words left his mouth when they saw a jeep headed their way. Moss arched an eyebrow at the pilot and asked, "What the hell did you do now, Captain?"

Skip could only shake his head as they watched the jeep approach. A moment later, the driver came to a stop directly in front of them. The MP riding shotgun climbed out and motioned towards the seat he just vacated. "Captain Colchord, if you could please come with us, sir." It wasn't a request.

Skip turned to Moss and shrugged as he walked over to the jeep. "Your guess is as good as mine, Sarge."

Captain Colchord stared in stunned silence at the lineup of officers standing in front of him in the mission briefing room. In addition to the Lion, there was a major, two captains, and a flight officer (technically a non-com, but an officer nonetheless.) All wore wings on their lapels. It was one of the captains, however, that had elicited his reaction.

"Captain Colchord, may I introduce Major Owen Anderson, Captain Patrick Lars and Flight Officer Frank Schildiner," said Col. Pollard in an even tone. "I believe you know Captain Stark."

"Gentlemen, ma'am," was all he could muster as a response. Suzie showed no sign of emotion.

Col. Pollard motioned to the map on the wall behind them. "Captain Colchord, you're being recruited for a top-secret intruder mission. Major Anderson will be piloting a P-61 fitted with an advanced radar system, which will be operated by Capt. Lars. This system will allow them to navigate difficult terrain in total darkness and to locate a specific target. Their plane will be armed with bombs and rockets to take out that target."

The giant mission planning map detailed all of Western Europe from the British Isles to the Eastern border of Germany and south to the northern parts of Italy. Pins on the map marked Allied air bases and planned targets, and yellow threads stretched from one pin to another to map planned attack and patrol routes. Skip noticed a single red thread that stretched from the pin indicating their current base in Belgium and terminated at another pin deep in the Bavarian Alps.

"Permission to speak, sir?" asked Colchord. The Lion merely sighed, which Skip took as tacit permission. Pointing at the map, he continued, "That's a long haul for a P-61, sir."

Captain Stark spoke up. "We'll be equipping both P-61s with drop fuel tanks, Captain. Those will extend the combat range enough to make it to the target and back."

"Both, ma'am? We'll be flying almost four hundred miles behind enemy lines with just two planes? That sounds like a suicide mission to me. The Luftwaffe still patrols German skies."

"Secrecy and timing are of the utmost importance," answered Suzie. "We're confident that the advanced radar capabilities will allow the planes to fly low enough to avoid most enemy aircraft. And one of the planes will be flying cover for the main attack plane. It's risky, yes, but possible."

"It sounds more reckless than risky, ma'am." Skip paused before smiling broadly at Suzie specifically. "So I'm definitely in."

☆ ☆ ☆

The sun hung low in the cold winter sky as Skip checked over his plane. The 'Windy City Widow' looked as good as new as it was being prepped for tonight's mission. Moss' crew worked around the clock for the past forty-eight hours repairing the damage to the rear fuselage. Peering into the refurbished R/O compartment, Skip noticed the radar scopes looked bulkier than normal.

"This the new radar set-up, Sarge?"

"Yes, sir. And you should see the antenna in the nose up front. Some serious high tech stuff."

Skip walked around towards the front of the plane and found Suzie staring up at the nose art.

"I'm not sure exactly how I feel about this, Skip, but I guess maybe I'm flattered?"

"Ah, yeah, about that…"

"A bit busty, isn't she? I mean, my bosom isn't quite so ample as all that, now."

"Artistic license," came Moss' voice from beneath the plane.

Suzie couldn't stifle her laugh. "Oh, Skip, it's so good to see you again." She moved towards him to wrap him in a hug.

"Suzie, let's talk when I get back," said Skip as he kept her at arm's length. "I need to focus on this mission tonight."

"OK," replied Suzie softly. "I… I understand."

Skip saw Major Anderson wave him over to his own plane parked next to the 'Windy City Widow'. She bore the name 'Domino Lady', and a portrait of a striking, gun-toting blonde woman adorned the nose. She wore a sexy white evening gown, a cape, and a domino mask. He also noticed a handful of swastika and train kill markings up there, along with a number of bomb mission markings. Major Anderson and his crew had been busy down in Italy.

"Let's go over this one more time, Captain, just to make sure we have everything buttoned down." The major pulled out his navigation map and spread it out on the hood of a jeep. "Once we reach the mouth of this mountain canyon here, we'll make our run. The train we're targeting will be crossing this bridge here at a specific time, so we only have one chance at this. If we miss, whatever it is that's on that train that Uncle Sam wants blown up doesn't get blown up. That means Jerry wins. It's that critical. Are we clear on this?"

"Crystal clear, sir. We'll get that train."

"You let me worry about the train, Captain. I just need you to keep Jerry off my ass long enough for me to hit it."

"Understood, sir," answered Skip.

Capt. Lars chimed in. "Once we're in the mountains, Skip, you'll have to listen closely to your R/O. These new radars our planes are carrying will allow you to avoid the terrain, but only if you work together. One misstep and you'll fly right into the canyon wall."

"Who will my R/O be, sir?"

"Captain Stark is working on that as we speak, Skip," said Major Anderson. "She said she had the perfect candidate. Your R/O will know enough to help you intercept bogeys, but that's about it. Leave the targeting and attack run to Pat, Frank and I."

They went over the plan several more times, discussing potential complications and planning last-minute contingencies. By the time everyone felt comfortable with their preparations, the sun had dipped below the horizon and its dying rays painted the clouds fiery hues of orange and red.

Major Anderson gathered both aircrews and ground crews together for one last inspirational speech. But Skip passed through all of it in a haze. Thoughts of Suzie distracted him, and only being in the cockpit of his plane could cure that.

With all the final preparations done and all the pre-flight lists checked off, it was finally time to mount up and take off. Skip climbed into the cockpit to find his gunner already strapped in and ready to go.

"A bit eager are we, Mick?"

"Yes, sir, but I'll be fine. R/O is all buttoned up in back, too, so we're ready to go."

"Well isn't my crew just the perfect picture of efficiency," said Skip with a smile.

'Domino Lady' and 'Windy City Widow' taxied to the runway together and took off in perfect formation. Wheels up, they turned East and aimed their noses towards Germany.

Skip keyed the intercom to find out who was riding in the back. "Pilot to R/O, you copy?"

"Copy you loud and clear, Captain," came a decidedly feminine voice. "Hope you don't mind me tagging along, Skip. Couldn't find anybody better qualified to work this radar than me."

"Suzie?! Are you nuts? We'll get court martialed for this!"

"If we pull this off, we'll be heroes, Skip. They don't court martial heroes. Besides, I know this system better than anybody else available. I helped test it, after all."

Colchord turned to glare up at Mick. "You knew about this, didn't you?"

Mick stared straight ahead wide-eyed and white-faced. "Just following Sgt. Moss' orders, sir!"

"Conspirators! I ought to bail out now and leave you both to your fates!"

"Focus, Captain," said Suzie. If he didn't know better, he could swear she was enjoying herself.

Colchord fumed for the next few hours as they infiltrated deep into Germany. They flew low and slow to avoid radar detection from ground units.

But hiding from radar equipped night fighters would require luck. As they neared the mountains that hid their target, their luck ran out.

"Contact, Skip," Suzie said a bit too loudly into the intercom. "Bogey at nine o'clock!"

"Copy that." They were following strict radio silence protocol, so calling over to notify the other plane was out of the question. But Capt. Lars surely would have picked the contact up, too. Skip moved slightly ahead of 'Domino Lady' and waggled his wings, and Major Anderson responded with a wing waggle of his own in acknowledgement. "All right, Suzie, talk to me. Let's hunt this Jerry down." He released his nearly empty drop tanks and moved to intercept.

The bogey clearly saw them coming. He countered every move they made to vector in on him. Only a radar-equipped night fighter could be this precise. Skip's only hope was to draw him away from 'Domino Lady' and engage him in a gunfight.

"Two thousand feet dead ahead, Skip, coming in at forty-five degrees. He's… Oh hell! Two more contacts dead ahead!"

Skip saw all three planes in front of him in the moonlight now. A Ju 88 sprouting dipole radar antenna from its nose and a pair of Me-109 fighters flying piggyback. In close formation, the trio of planes presented a single radar cross-section. But now that both fighters broke formation, all three planes became visible on Suzie's scopes. Tricky bastards! One of the Messerschmitts made straight for them, while the other dove down towards 'Domino Lady'. Laden with ordinance on her wing racks, she was a sitting duck unless she could make it to the relative safety of the canyon. Colchord doubted the German planes were equipped to fly that gauntlet.

"Hang on tight. I'm going to try something reckless. Mick, stay ready on your trigger and fire whenever you see anything in your sights."

Skip rolled the 'Widow' over onto her back and made an inverted dive towards the Ju 88. If he could knock that out of the sky quickly, the fighters would be almost completely blind.

"That fighter is moving in on our six!"

"Don't worry, Suzie, it's all part of the ride." Skip watched with satisfaction as the Eighty-Eight sensed his attack and broke into a sharp right hand turn away from the P-61. Counter to what the Germans expected, Skip broke hard left. The Me-109 on his tail had turned right in an attempt to get inside and line him up for a shot, but now the 'Widow' was temporarily out of sight.

Major Anderson broke radio silence. "We could use some help down here. We're taking fire."

"Hands are kind of full up here, right now," Skip responded. Switching to the intercom, he asked, "Talk to me Suzie. Where are our dance partners?"

"They are coming around from opposite directions, Skip. They're both moving to get behind us. The Me-109 is turning tighter than we are, though. He'll definitely get the drop on us if we don't do something."

"That's what I want," replied skip with a grin.

The Me-109 took a wild high-deflection shot hoping to get a lucky hit, and Mick returned fire with the dorsal turret. Skip barrel rolled the 'Widow', dropping airspeed without cutting the throttle. The German fighter zoomed by and turned sharp to get back in behind them. Unfortunately for Jerry, he'd been maneuvered directly into the flight path of the Ju 88.

"Oops," said Colchord, and he smiled as the two German planes desperately tried to evade. They almost succeeded, but the tip of the Messerschmitt's right wing clipped the bigger plane's left engine. The Ju 88's prop chewed up the fighter plane's wing before it was itself destroyed by the impact. A prop blade from the disintegrating engine sliced through the wing of the Eigthy-Eight and split open the fuel cell housed there. The resulting explosion engulfed the entire left side of the plane. Skip saw one person bail out of the Eighty-Eight as it went down, but he too burned with fire as he fell. No chute ever opened.

"Suzie, where's the fighter?"

"Off my scope, Skip. He must have gone down, too."

Skip keyed his radio. "Hang on 'Domino Lady', the cavalry is coming." With both engines wide open, the 'Windy City Widow' raced towards the mouth of the canyon. He was relieved to hear Major Anderson's voice respond.

"Copy that, 'Windy City'. Don't spare the horses."

About a mile into the canyon, Skip spotted wild streams of tracer fire arcing back and forth in the darkness. As he drew closer, he saw 'Domino

Lady' rolling and swerving and pulling every other evasive maneuver in the book in an attempt to shake loose the Me-109 on her tail. With wings loaded full of bombs and rockets, it took no small amount of skill to fly the P-61 like that. But the Me-109 was far more nimble, and despite taking fire from the 'Lady's' dorsal turret, the fighter whittled away at the bigger plane with its own machine guns and centerline cannon. Anderson's plane trailed smoke from its dead right engine, making Skip marvel even more at the Major's piloting.

He was able to maneuver in behind the German plane without being noticed, but before he could get within range, shells from the Me-109's 20 mm cannon scored a direct hit to 'Domino Lady'. Her central ammo magazine exploded, and fire spewed out from every orifice. "Oh damn! Bail out! Get out of there," Skip yelled into his radio.

Mick blasted the German with the turret machine guns as the fighter tried to pull away, striking the Me-109's engine. Oil sprayed from under the cowling and coated the fighter's flat-paneled canopy. Blinded, the pilot had no chance to see the rocky outcropping that intersected his flight path. The granite pillar struck the plane's wing root, and the Messershmitt cartwheeled to the canyon floor.

The 'Lady' maintained a level flight for a few moments, but the entire plane was now an inferno. Someone on board her keyed the radio mic, but only screams came across Colchord's radio. The transmission was cut mercifully short as the burning P-61 smashed into the wall of the canyon.

Skip stared back at the burning stain on the granite cliff face, too stunned to say anything.

"Focus, Skip!"

Suzie's warning jolted him back to his current situation: the canyon walls were now reaching out to smash his plane, too. With a reflexive jerk on his control yoke, Skip narrowly avoided impact. He now focused solely on the darkness around him. "Talk to me, Suzie!"

With Suzie watching her scope and calling out instructions, he managed to weave his way through the twisting canyon. The tense, adrenaline filled minutes seemed like hours. Finally, Suzie called out over the intercom, "Contact, two miles directly ahead. That's gotta be the bridge."

"And right on schedule," Skip replied. He could see the steam billowing from a locomotive engine as it approached the bridge. Colchord passed over the target and pulled his nose up to loop back over for an attack run. As he rolled inverted, he saw the train start crossing the bridge below him. As he was nosing over into his dive, he noticed a stream of tracer fire arcing towards him from the dark sky above.

He couldn't evade without aborting his attack, and he wouldn't get a second opportunity at his target. He committed to the dive and winced as he both heard and felt the shells hitting the 'Widow' like a continuous hailstorm of destruction. The right engine died in spectacular fiery fashion. G-forces pushed him back hard into his seat, but he lined up his nose with the steam billowing out of the train's engine. "Let 'em have it, Mick!"

Mick opened up with the P-61-s entire arsenal, and his aim proved true. The shells impacted the engine's boiler, and the entire locomotive exploded in a gout of steam and flame. Skip evaded the brunt of the destruction, but the already-damaged Me-109 that was diving down on his tail wasn't so lucky. With one wing already clipped short from the impact with the Eighty-Eight, the German fighter couldn't maneuver quickly enough and was shattered by the blast. The flaming remains of the fighter crashed into the train cars following the destroyed engine, finishing the job the 'Windy City Widow's' guns started.

The entire crew erupted into cheers. Skip circled the smoking ruins of the bridge to confirm complete destruction of their target. The remaining cars of the train plunged off the destroyed section of the bridge and plummeted to the canyon floor hundreds of feet below. No person or thing, whatever their target was, could have survived. "Mission accomplished, boys and girls," said Skip. "We may avoid that court martial after all."

As the 'Windy City Widow' rose into the night sky, she began to shudder. "Skip, what was that," asked a clearly nervous Mick.

Colchord scanned his instruments. "Uh oh," he said. "Left engine is overheating." As if on cue, their remaining engine sputtered. "That's not going to last much longer. We gotta bail out; there's no place to land in this canyon." No sooner had he said that, the left engine coughed and went dead. "Time to hit the silk, gang!"

☆ ☆ ☆

He awoke in total darkness on the ground of a rocky mountain field. His deflated chute engulfed him, and as he fought to get free he heard a familiar voice.

"That you, Skip?" came a decidedly feminine whisper.

A curvy female form was silhouetted against the moonlight for a moment before moving towards him with a slight limp. The snub-nosed revolver she held in her hand moved back and forth as she scanned the darkness for enemies. The first thought to cross his mind wasn't relief, but surprise at her having a gun. "You can take the girl outta Chicago…"

His knees buckled as his head started spinning. Or was it the ground that was spinning? He felt a warm body at his side supporting him as he struggled to regain his senses. Her flight leathers creaked in the silence of the night, and she smelled like aviation fuel and beautiful.

"Steady on, Skip," he heard her say. "We have a long walk home."

☆ ☆ ☆

The bartender flipped his towel over his shoulder. "Decades later, a hiker found the crash site in the mountains. Most of the plane was destroyed, but the salvage team managed to save this one piece. Dad hung it here behind the bar in memory of his father's bravery during the war."

The customer pushed his empty dinner plate away and finished the last of his beer. "Did they make it back?"

"Well, now, that's a whole different story all together. You come back for dinner tomorrow night, and I'll tell you that one."

The salesman smiled. "You have yourself a deal, my friend." As he got up from the bar he paused and took one last glance at the portrait of the 'Windy City Widow' on the metal panel. "So, that's what Suzie Stark looked like, huh?" He gave an admiring whistle. "Wow, she was a hottie."

"Hey now, be careful," said the bartender as he arched an eyebrow playfully at his customer. "That's my grandmother you're talking about."

The End

Discovering History

Being an aviation nut, I had an absolute blast writing this story. Even more fun than writing it, however, was researching it. One of the requirements for the story was to keep it real. So this meant no super soldiers zipping around with rocket packs, no glowing supernatural amulets, and certainly no Nazi dinosaurs (sorry, Tyrannosaurus Reich, maybe next time...) More importantly, this meant that everything we included in the story had to be supported by actual fact.

I found and absorbed dozens of books, articles, and videos about not just the P-61 Black Widow, but about night fighters in general. I even incorporated my memories of conversations with a WASP I met and befriended years ago. I learned about the capabilities—and limitations—of the radars of the era. I marveled at the desperate-yet-resourceful tactics of the Luftwaffe late in the war. And, ultimately, I came away impressed with the bravery of American air crews as they fought and died in the skies over Europe.

This tale is the result of all that research. It's not necessarily 'based on a true story' or 'ripped from the headlines', but every element of the story is made of factual bits and pieces. While there may be no record of the Luftwaffe flying a spotlight equipped P-38 Lightning night-fighter, for example, there were American night fighter units that did fly such P-38s, and there are records of the Luftwaffe flying captured Lightings.

And there really was a fly-off between the British Mosquito and the American Black Widow to determine which plane would equip the American NFS units in Europe. It even involved a Northrop test pilot training the USAAF pilots and the 'tweaking' of a pair of Pratt & Whitney engines. That story seemed more like it was ripped directly from the adventure pulps rather than the other way around!

The one element that strayed furthest from reality was having the WASP flying on the final combat mission. While many of the WASP pilots were every bit as capable as their male counterparts, no American woman ever flew on a combat mission in WWII. But I did want to honor the efforts of the valiant WASP pilots, and my co-writer Jeff was pushing to expand Suzie's role in the story, so we just had to put Suzie on that plane. Consider it a bit of artistic license.

We could have filled an entire novel with the tidbits and anecdotes we uncovered in our research, but alas, we had to pare all that down to the story you have in front of you. I sincerely hope we succeeded in entertaining you and maybe even piquing your interest in the fascinating P-61 Black Widow. Do some research of your own, and you may also discover some fascinating and enjoyable pieces of history.

ANDY FIX—first discovered heroes such as the Lone Ranger, Conan, Tarzan, John Carter, and Doc Savage as a child. Many years later, he would come to realize that all of these characters originated in pulp magazines. Since then, Andy has been a fan of all things Pulp, and he is very excited to be writing New Pulp adventures.

Andy is currently working on a New Pulp novel featuring Sir Axel the Axe, Knight of the Round Table, an original character of his own creation.

For updates on Andy's writing projects, you can follow him on Twitter (@ AndyFixWriter) and on Facebook (facebook.com/Andyfixwriter).

From Point 'A' to Point 'B'

A pilot once told me there is a big difference from flying a plane and fighting in one. It becomes a study in risk and necessity pitted against the cautious precision that all pilot have drilled into them by flight instructors. Controlled chaos probably comes closest, and war is the great ravening beast of that principle. Where you are taught all the proper ways to live and fly in flight school, you have to adjust to the new reality of air combat where safety is the only thing not guaranteed. There are precedents in civilian air races with high speed maneuvers pushing man and plane as far as they will go. They are dangerous but safe to a point.

Much like fighting in war, boxing or falling in love.

When you're a writer, there is always a story in man's endeavors. Being in a war or piloting a plane are both rich fuels for the prop driven fiction engine of the pulps. There is always a before and after, in war and in love. The getting from point 'A' to point 'B', that's the interesting part that brings to life dry history and events. You will know the names of people and place in the story long after it is in the books and part of history. They were the guys and gals you saw every day as you worked in your unit, fought, lived in a war. You will remember them, the sights and the sounds of it for the rest of your life. Whether you were in the seat with a stick, or on the ground turning a wrench.

It's the difference between flying a plane and fighting in one.

JEFF FOURNIER- is an Ohio native who has been writing fiction and non-fiction since he was in college. An avid reader of Science Fiction and Fantasy, he discovered Robert E. Howard and H.P. Lovecraft early on and was a fan of the stories they spun. In his spare time he has tried to keep his hand in various creative outlets, writing non-fiction articles for SJ Games *Pyramid*, *Self-Reliance* Illustrated, as well as pulp fiction for Airship 27. Jeff can be found on Facebook at https://www.facebook.com/jeff.venture.

Missing in Malaysia

Robert Ricci

1937

"**W**ho let this rook in the game?" The pale faced pilot demanded. He bared his uneven, tobacco stained teeth. "He cleaned out my beer tokens!"

The object of his wrath was a handsome American aviator, decked out in a worn leather jacket, soiled tank top and a pair of aviator gloves that had been snipped at the fingertips. The muscular man sat stiff, emotionless. His stoic expression was unreadable. He appeared lifeless until his lips moved.

"I believe it's your call."

The angry British pilot let out a huff of air between his clenched teeth. He stared at the corpse like opponent in front of him, trying to get a bead on his intentions, but it was useless. The American's face refused to betray his thoughts.

"Your call." he echoed.

The RAF pilot slammed a menacing fist on the table, spilling his drink. His hands trembled as spittle flew from his mouth. "I fold." He snarled.

The square shouldered American remained silent, dropping his cards and curling the huge pile of money toward his end of the table. He didn't bother to count it as he folded the bills into his shirt pocket. As an afterthought, he threw a handful back on the table.

"Always a pleasure to engage you fine folks." He said, beginning to rise from his chair.

The American felt a pair of strong hands grip his shoulders and hold him in place.

"What gives!" he demanded.

The drunken Brit pointed at the man standing behind the rugged blond aviator. "My friend suspects you have been cheating!"

For the first time the American showed emotion. He smirked and turned over his hand. He had a pair of deuces scattered among the draw.

"I hardly think a jury would find me guilty of cheating with this weak hand. The only person guilty here is you my hasty friend. Take my gesture of

85

friendship off the table and have your friend release his grip, and I'll overlook this disrespect you've shown me."

The Brit's face deepened with color, a combination resulting from beer and anger. He drew back his fist and lashed out at the American.

The sturdy aviator was expecting the attack. He ducked and timed it perfectly. The intended blow missed him and landed harshly on the pilot holding his shoulders.

Before either Brit could react, the American rose from his chair and landed a vicious blow on the chin of his antagonist. The man was unconscious before he hit the floor. His friend roared with disapproval.

"You will pay for that!"

He charged at the American in a clumsy manner only to join his friend in slumberland, courtesy of a crushing whack upside the head.

The American relaxed, withdrew the rest of the money from the table and added it to his stash. He was about to leave the hangar bash when two more RAF recruits blocked his exit.

"Really?" he muttered, balling his fists in anticipation.

The Brits grinned wolfishly. They were staring past the beefy aviator. He felt a chill go down his spine.

"There are more of you behind me?" he guessed.

Before they could answer, a fresh pair of arms collared the American and held him stiffly. He braced himself for a blow that didn't come.

He felt the powerful arms release their grip on him, and before he could turn around to react, the men who had grabbed him were airborne hurtling toward the other two pilots.

Suddenly, the room filled with a savage howling as a whirlwind of activity took place. A small child-like figure had entered the fray. Streaks of grease ran down her face like war paint. Dressed in mechanic coveralls, and wearing green lensed goggles, the diminutive warrior began thrashing RAF pilots left and right. Her lengthy, strawberry colored hair whipping back and forth, she struck with merciless precision.

Practically foaming from the mouth, the deadly girl withdrew a shiny monkey wrench from her backside.

"Glimmer! No!" yelled the American. "You'll kill them!"

His partner ignored his request and proceeded to wave the iron weapon at the enlisted men around the room. Her teeth glistened in the light, and she appeared less than human.

Suddenly a gunshot rang out.

"That's enough!" a high pitched voice shrieked. "This will end now!"

The dazed Brits stared with thankfulness at the tall figure standing before them, his revolver smoking.

"Brass hats!" someone screamed.

The American and his female companion employed a ready stance.

"We didn't start this." The aviator proclaimed.

The authoritative Brit simply holstered his weapon.

"No need to debate the subject, Mr. Sparks. Simply put, we'd like to procure your services."

☆ ☆ ☆

A half hour later in the commander's office, the regal Brit introduced himself. "I'm Harry Staish."

The American nodded, wishing to hear out the commander's offer. Glimmer slumped against a wall, content to chomp on a stick of chewing gum. She hadn't bothered to remove the goggles. Her eyes were mostly concealed underneath them. The tip of her monkey wrench was still visible from the back pocket. It left a frightening shadow on the wall.

The well-mannered Brit sat back in his chair and dropped a manila folder on his desk. He opened it to expose a dossier on the American pilot.

"Says here your name is Clint Sparks, better known as Solution Sparks. Odd nomenclature wouldn't you say?"

Sparks shrugged. "Nicknames stick, I suppose. So what's this about needing my help? It's not like the Royal Air Force is lacking in pilots."

The lanky commander plucked at his mustache with a pair of manicured fingers. "Sometimes it's prudent to keep Her Majesty's Service from involvement in delicate matters."

Sparks' interest was peaked. "Sounds like you may be hinting at a mission?"

The Brit cleared his throat and then lit a cigarette. He shook the pack and offered one to Sparks but was declined. Glimmer held out a hand, but the commander ignored her request. She snapped her gum in disgust.

"Something of a search and rescue mission to be precise." Staish stated.

Sparks leaned back in his chair, mind spinning. "You're not talking about searching for that missing pilot Amelia.."

The Brit cut him off with an abrupt grunt. "No, half the civilized world has been searching for her since she disappeared a few months ago. Our situation involves a more delicate matter."

Clint Sparks allowed himself a brief smile.

"You're missing a spy!"

This time it was the commander who offered a stone faced response. "Actually a scientist. A geologist, to be precise. Professor John Thatcher of Oxford."

Sparks raised an eyebrow. "The volcano expert?"

The Brit nodded. "One and the same. Professor Thatcher was conducting a research expedition in Malaysia when his party went missing. The British Navy dropped them off in Perak, one of the Federated Malay States under British supervision."

"Don't you mean control?" Sparks retorted.

Ignoring the aviator's caustic remarks, the commander flipped open another folder with a photo of the Oxford professor.

Sparks glanced at it momentarily before sliding it back across the desk. "I'm familiar with the professor's appearance. His face has adorned many magazine covers."

Staish slapped another photo down on his desk. This one revealed a young woman, barely out of her teens.

"That's Kate Thatcher, the professor's daughter. She accompanied him on his trek."

Sparks stared at the photo. The girl was beautiful, her face full of wonderment. She was holding a stone of some type.

"She's heavenly." The Brit offered.

Glimmer fired off a deliberate raspberry to show her disapproval.

Sparks didn't bite. "What's that she's holding?"

The commander didn't bother to look at the picture. "A lump of coal .That's what they were searching for in Malaysia."

Sparks weighed this on his mind. "So a respected geologist and his daughter have gone missing during an expedition to uncover coal. What does that have to do with British intelligence?"

Staish sighed as he continued to fondle his handlebar mustache.

"Unfortunately, Mr. Sparks, they weren't the only ones hoping for a coal strike."

☆ ☆ ☆

Glimmer kicked open the door of their bungalow with a gust of anger. Sparks never averted his eyes from the papers he was studying. He had been through this before. He knew her teen angst was beginning to bubble.

"Let's hear it." He mumbled, pretending to flip a page.

The fiery haired girl scrunched up her nose and then stomped a mud caked boot to the ground. Sparks didn't care. The bungalow had a dirt floor.

"This mission stinks!" Glimmer pouted.

Sparks suppressed a smile. "Is that so?"

This was the opening the youth sought. She bombarded him with a barrage of verbal insults and various explanations of why they shouldn't accept Staish's offer. At one point Glimmer's Polynesian face turned purple.

Throughout the entire outburst, Sparks remained calm, nodding his head in the affirmative. Little did his companion know that he wasn't even processing her words. No, his thoughts were focused on recalling the lovely image of Kate Thatcher cuddling a heap of coal.

"Are you listening?" Glimmer demanded.

Finally, Sparks threw down the folder and sat up on his cot. He grabbed the young girl by the wrists to stop her tantrum.

"Let go!" the feisty youth insisted.

"I will when you stop ranting like a banshee."

Glimmer struggled from his grip. "I'm not ranting. I'm discussing."

Sparks made a cynical face. "That so? 'Cuz from my perspective, it was a lecture, not a discussion. Didn't Granny teach you any manners all those years you spent with her?"

Granny referred to Sparks' grandmother, Helena, the child's legal guardian.

"Don't you say nothing bad about Granny!" Glimmer threatened. "She warned me about you, Clint Sparks!"

Sparks arched an eyebrow. "That so?"

"And stop saying that! I hate that expression!"

Sparks was about to repeat his signature line, but he caught a feint swell of tears start to form at the corner of the girl's eyes. It was rare that she had removed the goggles. Something was frightening her.

"What's really bothering you honey?" Sparks asked in a soothing tone.

Glimmer collapsed on the cot next to him. She still wore the grimy coveralls. Her hands were covered with grease as she clutched at Sparks pillow. He said nothing, staring at the stain.

Finally, the trembling youth spoke up.

"I don't want you to leave me." She muttered in a whispering tone.

Sparks was taken aback. He hadn't expected this. Glimmer was only fourteen years old, the last ten years of her brief existence having been spent in the care of Sparks and his loving grandmother, Helena.

The American aviator had rescued the girl and her mother when she was a tot during a mission along the Polynesian coast. Glimmer's mother had been fleeing a refugee camp, her husband the murder victim of a vicious rebel takeover. The mother hadn't been much older than Glimmer was now. Sparks agreed to fly them to safety, but unfortunately, he hadn't noticed the young mother had also been injured in the invasion. Glimmer's mother had succumbed to her injuries during the flight to safety.

The rest of the story was simple. Sparks brought the little girl back to the good ole US of A where he delivered her into the welcome arms of his grandmother. Like, Glimmer, Clint Sparks had been raised without a set of parents, and Granny had done a fantastic job with him. Surely she was up to the task of raising a helpless little girl?

Recalling her assault on the RAF pilots, Sparks wasn't so sure about the helpless part anymore.

He threw a comforting arm around the young teen's shoulder.

"Where's this nonsense coming from? I don't want to hear any talk of me leaving you."

Glimmer wiped away a tear. "Okay, Clint, but I saw the way you looked at that girl's picture."

Sparks caught her intentional use of his first name. She rarely called him by it, preferring to refer to him as Sparks.

"Afi," he said, using her birth name, "You know that you and Granny are the only ladies in my life."

Glimmer smiled. "The garage boys talk, Sparks. I'm old enough to catch the drift of what they're babbling about. Seems you're quite the ladykiller."

Now it was Sparks turn to blush.

"Listen, honey, it's true that someday I might meet a special lady and settle down, but that won't change what's between us. You're my family. You always will be."

The sullen youth brightened at his heartfelt words. She sniffled and then grinned.

"What's so funny?" Sparks demanded, anxious to spur the conversation in another direction.

Glimmer began laughing uncontrollably. "I'm just thinking of something Granny told me about you."

Sparks intentionally pretended to be hurt.

"Surely, my loving grandmother would have nothing but praise and kindness when discussing her only grandson."

"That's just it." Glimmer chuckled. "On more than one occasion she has thanked the good Lord that there's only one of you, Clint Sparks."

Sparks let out a guffaw and playfully slapped at her arms.

"Funtime is over kiddo. You need to bundle down for the night. We leave for Malaysia at daybreak."

Glimmer tossed him the grease stained pillow.

"And go wash up!" the burly aviator demanded. "You're not getting inside my plane like that."

The fiery haired youth deliberately ran a grease covered finger across his cot before winking and departing the bungalow.

"Goodnite, honey!" Sparks called out.

His keen ears didn't catch her whispered reply.

"You as well Daddy."

After confirming the coordinates with Harry Staish, Sparks and Glimmer departed undercover of the early morning sunrise from the British compound. The pair were flying a modified Blackburn Shark, which Sparks had liberated from the Portuguese Navy. The thirty five foot bomber was intended to be manned by a crew of three, but the duo had managed its operation just fine on their own.

One of the first adjustments Sparks had made upon purchasing the plane was to convert the torpedo bay into a storage compartment designed for holding his inventory of import and export goods. Glimmer casually referred to this part of the ship as Smuggler's Bay. Sparks humored her, and had agreed to let the youth paint a flaming pineapple upon the side of the plane. She had done a pretty decent job of it, displaying an artistic flair for the brush. Sparks felt it had a settling effect in aiding their cover as merchants.

The only setback he regretted was that the vehicle could only maintain an atmosphere of 15,000 feet. This made them vulnerable to pirates and hostile countries. Sparks had compensated for that setback by installing a Lewis gun left over from World War I. Glimmer had assumed the role of tail gunner, christening the Lewis weapon as "Big Guy." The fiery haired youth had grown quite adept at handling the deadly device. Thankfully, she hadn't been forced to use it often.

Sparks yelled back to her. "Make sure Big Guy is greased and loaded. I'm expecting unfriendly visitors during this sojourn."

Glimmer flipped him a salute. "I check it every day, boss. Big Guy is ready to go, and so am I."

Sparks glanced back at the tiny figure, with her green lensed goggles and olive colored skin contrasted by the overloaded red dye she had colored her hair with. She looked like a circus performer. Granny had suggested she'd outgrow that stage, but Sparks didn't care. He liked her vivaciousness.

"Kiddo, you understand the danger involved in this mission?" he inquired. "Staish suspects the good professor may have stumbled into something big."

"Stumbled?" Glimmer shot back. "Or maybe something more nefarious?"

Sparks grinned wildly. "Granny did good. Your vocabulary is aces."

The youth rolled her eyes under the goggles. She was about to fire off some sarcastic remark when she was jolted in her seat.

"What the hell? " Sparks demanded.

Glimmer had recovered and was focusing maniacally as she swiveled in her pivot seat. "Don't look now, Sparks but we got company! Bogey on your flank."

Sparks reacted with lightning reflexes; diving the huge bomber downward in a tailspin. The skilled aviator fought against unconsciousness as he leveled the plane against the deep decent. Glimmer had anticipated the nose dive. She was strapped in, fingers flexing for action. She gripped the trigger on the Lewis as the enemy came into sight.

"Big Guy is locked and loaded!" She shrilled toward the cockpit.

Sparks didn't look back. Experience told him, the agile youth could handle the tail gun if necessary. The cautious pilot was more interested in who his attacker may be. The enemy pilot flew an unmarked plane, no flag colors nor insignias.

"Hold on kiddo!" Sparks screamed as he banked the Shark closer to his prey.

Glimmer was able to spot the pilot from her pivot position.

"I see him!" She bellowed. "It's a Nip!"

"Damn!" Sparks cried. He had suspected as much. British intelligence had warned that the Japanese Navy had been stockpiling a fleet of vessels in the Malay states. Their intentions were obvious. They were ready for battle. Invasion of Malaysia was imminent, and the British were unprepared. Great Britain had focused its strength on building the world's largest navy, but it was sadly lacking in air support, the RAF still being coddled in infancy.

"Hold off on that trigger finger, Glimmer!" Sparks ordered. "We do not want to be responsible for starting a war."

The girl never averted her gaze from the enemy, but she barked a reply. "Tough on that! This idiot fired first. Let me introduce him to Big Guy."

Sparks replied in an even tone. "Only if we have to. I'm going to try and outmaneuver him."

Glimmer released her finger from the trigger. "Your funeral, Sparks."

The American aviator ignored her sarcasm, instead focusing his concentration on giving his opponent the shift. The Japanese pilot remained steady, content to maintain visual contact but not close enough to engage in battle.

"He's not trying to dog me." Sparks wondered. "What is he waiting for?"

His answer didn't take long.

Glimmer's shriek forewarned his fears.

"There are half a dozen Nips in the rear view, Sparks. He was waiting for reinforcements!"

Sparks crooked his head to the left for a better view. He almost fell out of his chair. The Japanese fleet had boxed him in, three craft on each side.

"Unleash Big Guy!" he roared.

Glimmer didn't hesitate. She spun in her chair like a whirlwind, unloading a barrage of deadly bullets at their attacker, all the while bellowing threats and curses at the top of her lungs.

The athletic teen managed to frighten off the planes on the left flank of the Shark, but this only left them vulnerable to an attack from the right. Bullets sprayed against the metal of the bomber, many of them piercing its hull.

"We're hit!" Sparks called out. "Get your chute on now!" He demanded.

Glimmer ignored him, spinning around in frenzy; she continued pumping bullets toward the Japanese planes.

"Glimmer!" Sparks ordered. "I said get your chute on now!"

There was a brief pause. The teenager had never heard her mentor use such force when speaking to her. She knew he was serious.

"But what about you?"

Sparks didn't turn around. "Just bail now. I'll be right behind you. I'm going to drop now and bank to the shore. You'll have a few seconds to leap out and pray they ignore you."

"And you?" Glimmer inquired.

"Right behind you." Sparks said, tugging on his own chute. "Now go. Stay hidden in the jungle. Use your skills, I taught you to avoid the animals. Once I'm down, we'll figure a way to contact you."

Tears welled at the corner of Glimmer's eyes. She removed the goggles to wipe them away. "I'll make you proud." She stated.

Sparks allowed himself a smile. "I'm already proud of you." He grabbed the wheel. "Get ready on three."

Glimmer hesitated. She wanted to rush the cockpit and hug him, but she knew there wasn't time. "See you soon Sparks."

He mouthed the words "I love you" and then dropped the plane drastically. The Blackburn dived and rolled instantly away from the menacing fleet. He didn't have time to watch Glimmer bale from the plane, but the open door and her lack of presence let him know she departed.

Sparks held his breath until he saw her chute deploy. Only then did he allow his focus to return to the enemy. The Japanese had recovered quickly and were diving toward him now.

"That's it creeps, follow me." He begged. His intentions were to draw them away from Glimmer.

His wish was negated as one of the Nips spotted her chute descending and gave pursuit. Sparks cursed and veered toward the plane. He had no tail gunner to open fire. His only intention was to intervene between the Japanese pilot and his youthful companion.

"Don't touch her you filthy vermin." He yelled, knowing the pilot could not hear him.

The Japanese pilot briefly made eye contact with Sparks, an evil grin encompassing his face as he realized the American's intention was to avert his pursuit of the parachute. He flipped his head wildly and dove deeper.

"Damn you!" Sparks cursed. He had one chance to save Glimmer's life. It might cost him his own.

Sparks barreled his Shark above the menacing Japanese plane and then sprinted to the back of the plane as quickly as possible. He knew he had only a second before losing altitude. His mighty fingers gripped the trigger of the Lewis gun and he fired madly at the Japanese bogey.

"Meet Big Guy!" he bellowed. Unleashing hell upon the unsuspecting opponent. The Japanese pilot was caught off guard, his focus pinpointed on Glimmer's descending chute. He never knew what hit him as Sparks managed to narrow his attack on the gas tank. The Japanese ship erupted in flames before sputtering into the ocean.

Sparks allowed himself a second to gloat before he realized in horror that his ship was hurtling toward the water at breakneck speed. His only salvation came in the form of satisfaction as he saw Glimmer's chute glide toward the jungle growth out of harm's way.

"Good for you baby girl." He chuckled, closing his eyes and gripping the wheel as he spun out of control. The only question was whether or not he'd be splattered against the water or the trees.

The Japanese fleet veered away from the death bound plane, content with the satisfaction of their apparent victory. Had they remained in the vicinity a minute longer, they would have witnessed one of the most miraculous landings in aviation history.

Sparks had gripped the wheel with all his might, tendons bulging from his neck as he fought against blacking out. He knew he had one slim chance for survival. The dense jungle was out of the question, the mighty trees would shred his Blackburn to pieces. No, he opted for the impossible.

He planned a beach landing!

The Shark's velocity was way too fast for a standard landing. He had only one prayer. He intended to bank the plane off the mighty ocean waves and hope to skip like a rock across the ferocious waters and plant the vehicle in the heavenly sand.

"C'mon baby, don't let me down!" he begged, throttling the lever. His hands were white, icy pale as he held the stick with a death grip. The sound of the roaring ocean was powerful in his ears. He could feel the Grim Reaper breathing fetid air down his neck.

"Not yet." He pleaded, thinking of young Afi. By now the teen had landed safely in the jungle terrain. She was all alone, and he would not abandon her.

The Blackburn hit the first wave like a ton of bricks. Sparks had fastened his seatbelt but the force of the impact tore the straps from his body. He was hurled toward the glass window and hit it with a sickening crunch.

He felt his world turn black as he saw the thick plate glass window begin to crack, forming a spider web. Then his vision turned red. Blood flowed from his forehead into his eyes as he wobbled to his feet.

The thirty five foot vessel skimmed the water at breath taking pace, but didn't break apart. Instead it roared across the ocean, hurtling in a death knell toward the sandy beach. Sparks barely had time to cover his eyes as the plane struck another wave, this time hitting so hard the plane actually went airborne again.

Clint Sparks grit his teeth and held onto the back of his cockpit seat. He was blind from the thick gobs of blood that caked his eyelids.

"This is it." He thought as the rumbling behemoth spiked toward the sand. He would make it to land, but the real question was whether or not he could survive the impact. The final thought rushing through the young aviator's head was one of fear. Boy would Granny be angry if she saw him now.

But then he thought of Glimmer, all those years ago, frightened and orphaned in a strange country. After accepting responsibility for guardianship, Granny Helena had christened the young tot with her new nickname, more for the feeling of pride and adultness that young aviator Clint Sparks had emitted than an actual name for the young girl.

"There's a glimmer of hope for you yet, Clint Sparks!" the elderly woman had declared a decade ago.

Sparks didn't get to complete his thoughts as the vessel struck ground. The frightened pilot was hurled at the shattered glass. He felt his body crash against the thick window and then all went black.

✰ ✰ ✰

Glimmer studied the jungle terrain. It consisted of thick, dense vines and mud flats, making it impossible for motor vehicles. It didn't matter anyway. There was no fuel on the island. The popular mode of transportation was bicycle. It was becoming a trend in this part of the world. The clever Japanese had invaded China earlier this year with an army consisting of 50,000 troops stationed strictly on bicycles!

The rebellious youth shuddered, recalling her encounter with the evil Japanese airfleet. A single tear flowed down her cheek, as she remembered the valiant Clint Sparks coming to her rescue, as he had done a hundred times before. She rolled her parachute back into its sack and donned her lucky green goggles.

She was fortunate enough to locate a banana tree in the vicinity. The fruit wasn't ripe, but it would provide nutrition and more importantly, stamina. She peeled the banana, eager to devour it, but something rustled in the growth to her left. Before she could turn to confront the intruder, she felt the banana get snatched right out of her hand.

"Hey!" she protested.

The thief turned out to be a chimpanzee, native to the island. The small animal grinned at her and shook his head teasingly as he popped the stolen fruit between his jaws.

"That's mine, you little brat!" Glimmer protested, lurching toward the chimp.

The twitching monkey only proceeded to glide into the nearest tree as if spooked by something.

"You better run!" Glimmer threatened.

She allowed herself a grin before turning to search out another batch of the plentiful fruit, but before she did her keen hearing caught a sound of movement coming down the muddy path she had just departed.

"My footprints!" she whispered.

...caught the sound of movement...

She had intended to wipe them, but the appearance of the chimpanzee had thrown off her intentions. She now scowled with regret as she sought refuge from whatever was heading toward her.

The rising sound of several male voices could be heard just yards away. She could also detect the sound of rubber bouncing off the dirt fields.

"Bikes!" she screeched fearfully.

Within seconds she sprawled out in the tall jungle growth, desperate to spot the intruders. A shiver ran down her spine when her ears caught the familiar babble of Japanese soldiers howling orders at each other.

Glimmer knew she had only one chance. Imitating the fleeing monkey, she took to the vines and pulled herself up, hand over fist toward the thicker branches. She was almost out of sight when the first bullet tore a fragment of bark right beneath her feet.

The Japanese were firing upon her. She cursed her decision to dye her dark mane fiery red. It stood out in the glaring sunlight, making her an easy target for the sharpshooters.

The infantry advanced cautiously, discarding their bicycles to pursue her on foot. This only served to increase Glimmer's advantage. Years of climbing the ropes inside Granny Helena's horse barn had served to strengthen her upper body like that of a gymnast. She scurried higher into the trees, where the foliage was denser and the leaves provided more stealth.

The Japanese soldiers cursed wildly, unable to follow her into the tree. Spurred on by renewed courage, Glimmer slipped off her backpack and hurled the heavy chute toward the pursuers. Her aim was spot on as three of the Japanese soldiers collapsed from their perch, bellowing hollow threats as they watched the young teen depart.

Glimmer never looked back. She trained her ears to the sound of onrushing water. It was coming from up high. That could mean only one thing. She was nearing a mountainous waterfall.

☆ ☆ ☆

Evading the Japanese hunters proved easier than navigating through the aerial density of the jungle terrain. Several times, she lost her balance on tree limbs, only to hang on precariously from her fingertips. The deafening roar of the waterfall increased as she got nearer and this renewed her with a sense of vigor. The athletic teen hustled her way through the branches, enduring a few scrapes and bruises, but soon she no longer heard the menacing yelps of her Japanese aggressors.

She had given them the slip.

She stopped to devour a hard banana, almost choking on the fruit. Her dry throat ached from thirst, but she knew relief was in sight. She allowed herself a gigantic grin as she cleared through a patch in the undergrowth and finally glimpsed a view of the magnificent waterfall. Sparks would be proud, for sure.

Her reverie was interrupted suddenly by the sound of a motor vehicle.

"Here? On this island?" she gasped.

Glimmer rubbed her eyes in disbelief from her perch in the tree tops. Suddenly barreling from the tropical brush came a military truck. The insignia was unmistakable. A swastika!

"Oh no." she thought. "First, Nips and now Krauts!"

She arched back into the shadows, anxious to avoid being spotted by the oncoming party. The truck was occupied by two soldiers, dressed in haunting black uniforms that could only signify one thing…Gestapo!

The fiery haired Polynesian shivered as she retracted even further into the foliage, draping large green leaves over her head. How she wished she had adorned an aviator's hat like Sparks possessed. The teenager glared at the sun. Finally, she had caught a break; it was almost sunset in the jungle, and she had already obtained higher ground.

"What would Sparks do?" she muttered, removing the goggles for a better view of the Nazis.

She watched, mesmerized as the rugged truck circled the waterfall before departing around a bend. She waited until the last sound of its engine ceased before she relaxed her guard and slipped down from the trees. The sun was setting fast. She planned on gathering drinking water and then resuming her position in the safety of the trees.

"Assess the situation, prepare a plan, and then don't hesitate to act." She told herself, recalling the usual advice Clint Sparks dished out before each mission. The fiery haired teen shook her head wildly. "That so?" she mumbled to no one in particular.

☆ ☆ ☆

Everything was pitch-black. Clint Sparks tried to scan his surroundings, but he couldn't see.

"I'm dead." He thought.

After a moment, the dazed aviator realized his eyes had been swollen shut from caked blood. With a little effort and a lot of pain, he forced himself to pry the lids open.

"Ouch!" he cursed. His head throbbed. There was a knot on the top of it the size of a golf-ball. He gently tapped it with a forefinger. "Well at least my thick skull came in handy for something."

The American aviator scanned his surroundings. He had somehow crash landed upon the sandy beachfront. The nose of the Blackburn Shark was embedded in the sand, but the propeller wasn't snapped. With some spit and polish she might fly again.

Climbing from the cockpit, Sparks glanced around his surroundings. He wasn't nervous. Scouting reports had shown this portion of the island to be non- inhabited. As he landed in the soft sand, his body quivered with pain. His shoulder was dislocated. Sparks removed his tie and placed it between his teeth. He flared his nostrils twice and then without hesitation, rammed his wounded shoulder into the edge of the wing.

He felt a pop and then his arm went numb, but within seconds, he could tell he had knocked his shoulder back into place. He spat the tie onto the blazing sand. He withdrew a canteen from the ship and splashed a few drops on his face to clear the dried blood from his eyes.

"That's better." He told himself unconvincingly.

Within minutes, Solution Sparks had managed to remove a large tan tarpaulin from his cargo bay and covered the length of the Shark with it. This would protect the plane from aerial view if any of the Japanese birds decided to wonder if he had survived the tailspin.

Sparks studied the sunset. He didn't have much time. His one thought was to find Glimmer wherever she may be.

He closed his eyes and tried to remember the descent of her chute. The vivid memory of bullets emanating from the Japanese attackers caused him to snap open his eyes with fear, but he forced himself to focus and soon he remembered spotting the Polynesian girl drifting toward a volcano or something like one.

"More likely a cinder cone." He told himself. He visualized the direction of the cone and pulled a compass from his vest pocket. He had the correct coordinates, now all he had to do was survive a jungle trek. "Piece of cake."

Gathering up supplies from the wreckage into his backpack, he steered himself in the right direction and began the long dredge toward recovering his ward.

Sparks fought off gnats and other bothersome insects as he shambled, zombie-like through the dense jungle. He was running on impulse, every bone in his body aching for rest, but he trekked on with determination. Every few miles, he pulled out a tiny heart shaped pendent containing a snapshot of Glimmer which had been taken at a county fair when she was ten. The angelic face had a smile for the ages. She had won two of the events that day, both against male competition; some a few years older than her, but Granny Helena had passed on all the secrets she had imbued on Sparks himself decades earlier.

Snapping the pendent shut, Sparks marched on silently, a new vigor in his step. His sense of urgency increased with every fade of sunset. He didn't stop to eat; only occasionally imbibing from the water canteen. He was saving his rations for the girl.

After hours of trudging through mud splattered terrain, his ears perked up at the sound of rushing water.

"A waterfall!" he proclaimed.

Surely, Afi would have the sense to head in the same direction? The American aviator felt a surge of new energy flow from his limbs, and his strides became longer. He began to trot and then eventually sprint, mindless of his surroundings. This proved to be unwise, as he had let his guard down.

His eyes saw the net seconds before he sprung the trap, but it was too late. Solution Sparks was jerked off his feet and catapulted straight up in the air, his flailing limbs tangled up in a mesh netting.

"Damn it!" he cursed.

His expected his angry rhetoric to fall upon deaf ears, but he was surprised when shadows emerged from the tall brush, ushering in a sense of forebode. Before he could ponder his situation, he was struck senseless by a bamboo staff.

☆☆☆

Sparks awoke to peer into the eyes of an indigenous native. The fierce warrior was dressed sparsely in a loincloth and animal felt coverings acting as shoes. His massive torso revealed several battle wounds. This man had been tested and survived. He would be a formidable foe. The warrior was barking threats into the aviator's ears.

"Easy buddy!" Sparks pleaded. "My head feels like the fourth of July."

The native only grunted and turned back to his companions. Like him, their faces were adorned with bright war paint. They, too, sported various scars.

"I don't suppose you fellows speak English?" Sparks inquired, knowing full well they didn't. He tried greeting them in several other languages, but got the same response. "Well, anyway, welcome to the twentieth century."

Suddenly, Sparks realized he was suspended upside down from a thick limb, his feet bound together by rough vines.

"Salutations!" he grumbled.

The three warriors stared at him with ferocious intensity and then huddled together like football players deciding the next play.

"This doesn't look promising." Sparks mumbled to no one in particular.

The natives continued to ignore him, finally breaking free from their conference. Huge grins spread across their faces as they pointed madly at the bound aviator.

"Listen, guys, why don't you cut me down from here and we can have a doubles match. I'll take gruesome on my side." Sparks joked.

As if they heard him, one of the warriors produced a large machete and slashed at the rope holding him. The thick woven strands burst apart and Sparks hurtled to the ground. He felt his shoulder separate again.

"Damn!" he bellowed. "You guys are ruining my chances of winning the horse shoe tournament this summer! Granny won't like it."

The lead warrior ignored his rantings, choosing instead to gift the loud mouthed American with a perfectly placed kick to the ribs. Sparks clenched his teeth as the breath escaped his lungs. His feet were still bound, but his hands were free. He scooped up a pile of dirt and hurled it into the native's face.

Enraged, the warrior clawed at his eyes, before unleashing a barrage of kicks at Sparks. This served to quiet the feisty pilot down. The other two natives quickly restrained his hands with more vines.

"Okay fellows this has gone long enough. I don't know why you boys are pretending to live in the stone-age, but I'm and American pilot and I demand you get me a radio so I can contact my superiors!"

This request only served to amuse the three warriors. They began to howl and chant as the final slivers of daylight faded away.

"Not a bright idea, guys." Sparks warned. "Sun's gone and you're screaming is only going to attract the wild animals. We'll be torn apart."

The natives only increased their chanting. The throbbing rhythm cascaded through the air worsening Spark's already massive headache.

"Listen, boys, we got off on the wrong foot. Cut the Halloween shenanigans and let me loose."

The warriors assembled brush and wood and began to light a small campfire. They lined up large stones to contain the flames.

"Again," Sparks warned, " the flame will probably attract more animals than it will frighten."

They ignored his verbal suggestions and within moments had a comfortable blaze stoking. One of the warriors screamed orders at a smaller man and he departed.

"I hope you sent him for a radio, not that it would help. Damn Brits told me this part of the island was unoccupied expect for maybe the Professor and his daughter."

The diminutive native returned shortly, carrying a familiar looking backpack. Sparks heart thumped wildly. He recognized the pack immediately. It was the one Glimmer had kept her chute in.

"Where did you get that?" he demanded.

The three natives huddled again. They kept staring at the American aviator and turning back to each other, baring their razor sharp teeth. It was obvious the men had filed down their choppers to give them a more frightful look.

Sparks gulped. The effect worked.

The leader, the man who had assaulted Sparks with the bamboo stick, released a victorious blood curdling scream before grabbing the pilot by the hair. Tremendous pain shot down Sparks' back. His head still throbbed from the original blow he had suffered during the Shark's crash landing. He clenched his teeth, determined not to show cowardice.

"Okay chief whatever your name is, this is your last chance. That pack belongs to my daughter and I demand to see her now!"

The warrior shook his head wildly. His skull was shaved except for a single streak of hair on top. It made him more menacing.

"Where is s..." Sparks began. His question was interrupted by a stone fisted backhander to the chin.

The native waited to see if Sparks would continue badgering him, but the airman thought wiser of it. He settled back to the ground, his chin dribbling scarlet blood. The warrior grabbed Sparks by the hair again and shoved the large satchel under his nose. He grunted twice wildly. Apparently, he wanted the American to peek inside.

"You shouldn't have! It's not even my birthday." Sparks managed hoarsely.

Undeterred, the warrior released his grip on Sparks' hair and waved the bag under the pilot's nose. A chill went down Sparks' spine.

"Oh God no!" he whispered.

Fearful that the warriors may have harmed Glimmer, the pilot summoned the last remaining bit of strength he had and sat up. A look of determination surfaced from his eyes.

"If anything has happened to Afi, I'll kill the lot of you!" he promised.

The warrior remained undaunted. Like a vaudeville act, he waved his hands over the satchel while continuing his menacing chant. The moonlight reflected off his war-paint, giving off an eerie glow.

Sparks struggled with his bonds, his face turned beet red. His frustration and anger had reached the boiling point. All he could imagine was what these vile savages had done to his little girl.

"I'll kill you!" he echoed.

With a burst of superhuman strength, Sparks ripped the vines from his wrists and snatched at the burlap sack. Caught off guard, the warrior was unable to maintain his grip. The bag was savagely ripped from his cabled hands.

With a sickening feeling in his stomach, Sparks tore open the straps to the bag and said a silent prayer as he unfolded the canvas and peered inside.

"Oh my God!" he shrieked after viewing the contents.

Numb, he dropped the pack and backed away in fear.

Laughing maniacally, the head warrior snatched up the tan satchel and reached inside. His hand withdrew a large black object. It was writhing in his grip. Whatever it was, it was alive.

Now exposed to the glow of the fire-light, Sparks settled back. His imagination had conjured up gruesome images of body parts, but now he was able to detect the true nature of the object.

"Giant beetles!" he thundered, edging away from the warrior chieftain. Sparks tugged at his ankle bonds.

The warrior held out the insect toward the frightened pilot, pincers first. The chittering bug had to be at least a foot and a half long.

"Get away!" Sparks cried, swatting at the chief's hand.

Undaunted, the massive warrior thrust the giant clawed beetle toward the pilot again.

"Okay, tall dark and ugly, I get it. You mean to kill me by slow poisonous death!" Sparks uttered, balling his fists. "Well you'll find Granny Sparks didn't raise no quitter!"

The American lashed out at the chief, knocking the giant beetle from his grasp. The stunned warrior lunged after the scuttling insect but it escaped into the freedom of the darkness.

Sparks unleashed a yelp and snatched at the burlap bag. The chief recovered in time to have a fierce tug of war.

"Oh no you don't" Sparks spat, tearing the satchel from the natives hands. Victoriously, he slung the tan pack with all his might into the darkness of the jungle.

The chief turned and watched the bag spiral into the dense thicket of brush. He then turned and stared at Sparks in bewilderment.

"Well what do you think of that?" the pilot demanded.

A youthful voice called from the darkness. "I think you just threw away your dinner, you numbskull!"

Sparks couldn't believe his ears. His mind was playing tricks on him.

"Glimmer?" He shouted.

☆ ☆ ☆

Despite the darkness of the midnight hour, Glimmer wore her shiny green aviator goggles. Absurdly, this wasn't the most peculiar part of her outfit. Gone were the mechanic overalls, replaced by a home-made sarong draped around her slender hips. Her torso was covered by two sea shells held together by seaweed strands. To top off the ensemble, a plume of colorful feathers adorned her native head piece.

"Have you lost your mind?" Sparks wondered incredulously. He started to approach the young girl, who towered above him aloft on a wooden throne carried by four more of the indigenous natives. Sparkling beads shimmered in the moonlight around her neck. She still sported the fiery red hair that clashed with her Polynesian ethnicity.

Sparks felt a strong grip on the back of his collar. It was the native leader who had offered him the giant beetle.

"What now?" the aviator demanded.

The fierce warrior snorted wildly and then answered him in his own language. "Do not lay hands upon our goddess!"

Sparks was taken aback. "So you do speak English!" Then his jaw dropped. "Wait, what? Did you say goddess?"

The chieftain released his powerful hold. Sparks didn't hesitate; he spun behind the massive warrior and grabbed his neck in a powerful choke hold.

"Let the child go or I snap Big Chief Gruesome's neck!" he demanded.

The four natives holding Glimmer high above their shoulders did not flinch. They remained stolid awaiting a signal from their leader.

The chieftain didn't struggle against Sparks grip. The American had locked his fingers together against the man's neck and was applying enough pressure to prove he could carry forth his threat.

Finally, the chieftain spoke. "Tell me goddess, do all white men behave like this dolt?"

Glimmer threw back her head and released a thunderous laugh. "Oh, no, there is only one Clint Sparks, better known as Solution Sparks."

Sparks gingerly released his grip upon the powerful warrior. "I guess I'm late for the party." He mumbled.

Again, the energetic teen released a howl before instructing her escorts to lower her throne to the ground. By the pale moonlight, she looked much older. She was quickly becoming a lady.

Sparks rushed to Glimmer's side and hugged her fiercely. "Baby, you made it safely."

The young teen stared at her guardian's blood streaked face. "Apparently better than you did. What did you think you landed in some Hollywood matinee where the natives are cannibals?"

The proud American was at a loss for words. "Well, I .."

Glimmer waved a hand at his stuttering and began speaking to the natives in their own tongue. Sparks was mesmerized by the teen's grasp of communication. She had been in the United States for most of the past decade, only occasionally joining Sparks on an undercover mission, yet she spoke her native tongue fluently as if she had never left the islands.

He waited for her to finish the long speech and then inquired what she had told the chieftain.

"I told their boss you're okay." Glimmer summarized.

A huge grin surfaced on Sparks' face. "That so?"

"Yep." She shook her head. "Afraid of insects, really?"

Sparks smiled sheepishly. "I don't suppose you have anything else for a hungry traveler?"

☆ ☆ ☆

While they dined on bananas and figs, Glimmer filled in the blanks for Sparks. She told the pilot about the secret caverns behind the waterfalls that she had witnessed Nazi caravans disappear into. Sparks listened intently, eager to resume his search for the missing scientist. His thoughts once again drifted to the photo of the lovely Kate Thatcher.

"I haven't heard anything about the Professor or his daughter." Glimmer spoke as if reading his mind. "Our friends here were very receptive to the idea of helping us locate the expedition. It seems the few encounters they have had with the Japanese infantry have turned out bad."

Sparks couldn't believe it. "That's an act of war. These islands are under British protection!"

Glimmer feigned looking around. "I don't see no redcoats."

"We need to get out of here!" Sparks warned. "All this hoopla will attract the Krauts!"

Again, the teenager shook her head as if she were addressing a child. "No chance of being attacked at night. The nips and Nazis are frightened of the natives at night. They know their superior fire power means nothing against the native's knowledge of the lay of the land. The chief told me they have repelled any night-time sneak attacks with ease."

The warrior chieftain had remained quiet during the discussion, but now he couldn't hold his tongue. "You speak with great praise young goddess, but the night is brief my friends. The devils on their two wheeled vehicles will return at daylight seeking you, and the invaders venture daily from their stronghold. We must retreat to the safety of our village in order to protect our goddess."

Sparks bit his lips. "So you're still prattling on about Afi being a goddess?"

The youth pouted. "Hush, Clint Sparks! If these brave warriors have designated me as their goddess who am I to argue? Besides, I think it's flattering."

Sparks snorted. "Of course you do." He turned his attention to the chieftain. "You're right about one thing. If we don't find shelter soon, the goddess and all of us will be in deep trouble."

With one wave of his hand, the chieftain ordered his tribe to snuff out the campfire and pack up their belongings. The stealthy warriors moved swiftly, removing all evidence of their occupation. Within minutes, the group had set out for the safety of the native village.

☆ ☆ ☆

Clint Sparks rested comfortably on a bed of straw. The tribal shaman had patched up his cuts and applied a soothing lotion to his tired dogs. Laying back, arms behind his head, he puffed on a cigarette as Glimmer entered the hut.

"Put that stinking stick out!" the youth commanded. "You told Granny you would kick that nasty habit." Sparks reluctantly extinguished his smoke.

"Granny ain't here, kid! But, since I don't need an earful of your belly-aching, I'll snub this butt out."

Satisfied, Glimmer took a seat on the floor next to him. She sat cross legged, a stern look on her face. She had cleaned off the tribal makeup the warriors had dabbed her with.

"Now what?" Sparks demanded.

The restless teenager rocked back and forth, shaking her crimson colored hair wildly.

"Nothing." She stated, tersely.

Sparks knew better than to let it rest. "Cough it up, Afi. What do you want to tell me?"

The girl scrunched up her lips. "I was trying to figure out why the Krauts are here, so far from their homeland. I mean, we all knew the Japs had a presence here, but Germany? That had me thinking."

Sparks sat up stiffly, eager to see where the girl's thinking was headed.

"Not just the Germans," Glimmer continued, "But also our good pal, the missing Professor Thatcher, expert on all things coal."

The American aviator focused on his young protégé.

"And you think there is a connection between his disappearance, and the emergence of Nazi supporters on this island?"

Glimmer nodded. "Too much of a coincidence." She uncrossed her legs and sprung up. "I batted it around with my new buddy, the chief, and we came up with a few ideas."

"That so?" Sparks spit.

The wild eyed Polynesian became animated. "For sure! You got this big shot scientist who works with coal on an island that lacks any motor vehicles. Then, you have these Germans driving around in a truck all day long. It got me thinking. Where are they gassing those buggies up? Not like there is a Shell Gas station around the corner."

Sparks' mouth dropped open. "Synthetic fuel!"

"And the man wins a prize!" Glimmer shouted. "Yeah, big chief says they have been here for months without any supply ships dropping by, yet the trucks continue to roll out from behind the waterfalls. They're making fuel."

Clint Sparks jumped to his feet also. "And the only raw material around here that could process that fuel has to be coal! This area is loaded with it. These guys must have got help from Professor Thatcher to create a batch of fresh fuel."

Glimmer was satisfied with that explanation, then a frown supplanted her smile. "Only question to be answered is about the professor."

"What about him?"

"Well it's obvious he is helping the dirty Krauts make their sauce. What I want to know is if he is doing it against his free will."

Sparks grimaced. "What you mean to say is, is the good professor a traitor?"

Glimmer didn't answer the pilot. Instead, she sprawled out on the floor, and decided to catch some shut eye.

☆ ☆ ☆

The morning flew by fast and furious. The natives refused to trek along with Sparks and Glimmer, but they did offer aid in the form of food and supplies. Transportation was out of the question. The pair would have to trek through the dense foliage under the oppressive jungle heat.

Cautious of the daily German patrols, the duo kept to the inner trail mapped out by the chief. The going was slow and laborious. Sparks hacked and slashed his way through the thickets aided only with a rusty machete the natives reluctantly had supplied. Glimmer protected her eyes from the sharp branches with her colorful goggles, but even the athletic teen was showing signs of depleted energy.

They cautiously followed the sound of the roaring waterfall, each cascading fall urging them to dig deeper into themselves to proceed. The plan was simple, get there by nightfall and infiltrate the camp under the pale moonlight.

"Ouch!" Glimmer yipped, her hair snagged on a low hung branch. Sparks turned and shot her a stern look. They had to maintain silence, but he didn't want to discourage the young girl's bravado.

"I told you that hair would be a problem." The pilot whispered. "What damn color is that anyway?"

"Red!" the exhausted youth piped.

Sparks shrugged. "If you say so. It's more purple than red."

Glimmer sighed and untangled herself from the branch. She prided herself on her independence, and any chance to push Sparks buttons pleased her to no end.

"Granny approves, and she has a lot better taste than you, flyboy."

"Okay, pipe down. Let me make myself clear. These Nazis have an agenda. That short tempered maniac they follow has bigger designs than just Europe. These guys don't mess around."

Glimmer halted, hands on her hips. "You have a point? Because today's not Sunday and I'm not in the mood for one of your sermons."

"Listen up kid. This is not one of your dime rag adventures. I need you to stay clear of that camp. It's dangerous."

Glimmer pretended her fingers were a gun and mocked shooting herself.

"How many times do I get this speech? Face it Sparks. I'm here, deal with it."

....they kept to the inner trail...

Sparks shot her a defiant look. "You're a real pain in my neck, Afi."

"The name's Glimmer. Remember, when we are on a mission code names only."

"Okay, okay, but just lay back and follow my lead. Professor Thatcher is an important man, and the Brits are counting on us to rescue him."

"And his daughter the princess," Glimmer added.

Sparks was about to retort, when they heard the familiar sounds of an engine approaching. "The Krauts!" He pushed Glimmer into the branches, hard.

The youth swallowed her tongue, and buried her head deep into the foliage. She hated to admit it, but Sparks was right, the fiery colored hair only served as a hindrance to a stealth mission. She would have to rectify that if they got out of this jam.

☆ ☆ ☆

As the German patrol scooted closer, Sparks got an idea. It was wildly insane but he was tired and his body still ached from the crash.

Without warning he emerged from the brush.

"Ahoy mates!" He waved, forcing himself to shape his face into the widest grin possible. He was careful to make sure his hands were in the air, and that he looked as harmless as possible.

The two Nazi soldiers slammed to a halt, the grill of their vehicle missing Sparks knees by a fraction.

They barked menacing words in German, but Sparks only continued to smile.

"How lucky am I?" He hollered. "Crash landed on this wretched island, and I thought I'd never see another face and now you two come along, my saviors."

The soldiers turned and snarled words at each other. It was apparent they were debating what to do.

"You two gents have any water?" Sparks inquired, mimicking swigging from a bottle. "This sun is hot as hades."

The driver glared at him menacingly. "Hades might be preferable."

Sparks ignored the hostile tone, instead feigning relief. "Thank goodness, my man. You speak my tongue."

The soldier removed his cap and wiped sweat from his hay colored hair.

"Curb your tongue!" He barked.

Sparks exaggerated fear and shuddered dramatically. "Please sir, I've been injured in a crash and I only seek your kind aid."

The German nodded to his companion who got out of the passenger side and quickly approached Sparks. The affable pilot held out his hand for a friendly shake. Instead he received a punch to the gut.

Sparks dropped to his knees. He peered into the jungle. No sign of Glimmer. The girl was too clever to reveal her location. He gulped a huge breath in relief.

"That wasn't very hospitable," he croaked, rubbing his aching midsection.

The aggressive soldier withdrew his pistol and aimed it at Sparks head.

"Whoah!" the airman protested. "No need for weapons."

The other Nazi had killed the engine and exited the vehicle. He ordered his partner to lower the weapon.

"Who are you?" The driver demanded.

Sparks rose slowly, cautious not to alarm the pair, and brushed the dirt from his trousers.

"Name's George Washington," he spouted, extending his handshake offering again.

Neither soldier caught the joke. They stood tense, sizing up the wounded pilot. Fortunately, for Sparks, the rough travel had left him with even more scrapes and bruises. He hardly looked like a threat.

"How about that drink now?" He pleaded.

The driver's eyes narrowed. It was obvious he intended harm. He nodded at his companion. Sparks heard the cocking of a pistol behind him. He closed his eyes, and prayed that Afi wasn't watching.

He heard a grunt and felt hot air on his neck. A second later, the other soldier toppled onto him, a blade imbedded deep into his spine.

Shocked, the driver lost his composure. He fumbled to withdraw his open weapon from its holster, but it was too late. Sparks had reacted swiftly, tackling the man around the ankles. He fell backward, striking his skull on the hood of his truck. He wouldn't be menacing anyone for a long time.

Sparks sprung into a crouch, wildly searching his surroundings. No one had witnessed the scene. His heartbeat raced as he craned his neck in search of his ward.

"Glimmer? Glimmer!"

Afi swaggered out from the foliage. It was obvious she was proud of her accomplishment. Sparks didn't condone murder, but in this case it was unavoidable.

"Thank you." he whispered.

The youth lifted her green goggles. The fear on her face was apparent.

She hugged Sparks fiercely. "I had to do it Clint."

He kissed her forehead. "I know baby, I know."

Glimmer was eager to put the incident behind her. "Now what?" she begged with just a hint of a sob.

Sparks stared at the two corpses with determination. He bent over and removed the cap off the driver and marched over to Afi. He tucked her long flowing hair into a knot and slipped the cap over it.

"You've got to be joking?"

There wasn't a hint of amusement on Sparks' face. "Get the rest of the· uniform on, Glimmer. We're not waiting for nightfall."

"Follow my lead." Sparks barked as they approached the gates of the German compound.

Glimmer snorted. She tugged at her oversized cap. She had substituted a pair of dark sunglasses for her familiar goggles, but her tiny frame betrayed her.

"You think this will work, Sparks?"

The American aviator shrugged as he pulled up to the gate. One single guard sat before the makeshift barrier. It was simply a huge tree branch designed to block the roadway. The Nazi looked pale in the torrid heat.

Sparks slowed to a crawl and snapped a curt salute toward the infantry man. Much to his relief, the bored soldier waved back lazily and removed the log from its holding. Afi simply sat still, head down as the pair drove the truck down the dirt road. Sparks looked back in his side mirror, but the guard was pre-occupied clumsily returning his burdensome log back to its berth.

"Piece of cake." Sparks snapped joyously.

Glimmer didn't answer. The youth's attention was drawn to the majestic waterfall that lay before them. Torrents of white foamy river water smashed against the rocks so loudly they couldn't hear each other.

"Now what boss?" the teen asked.

Sparks shrugged. "This is as far as the natives have seen them travel. Apparently, the truck just vanishes into the waterfall."

"Nonsense. The water is too deep. There is no place for them to drive to."

The brawny airman slowed down on the accelerator as he drew closer to the water's edge. "The chief swore they drove right into the waterfall. Magic he claimed."

Afi removed the cumbersome cap and threw it into the water in an act of disgust. "Revolting!" She muttered. "Look, Sparks, there's nothing ahead of us but this waterfall. If those guys drove around it, the chief would have known about it."

Sparks put the truck in park. "So do we get out and swim?"

"To where?"

"Exactly my point, this water is too powerful to swim in. We'd be crushed or drowned."

The aviator sucked in a lungful of air. "Put on your seat belt, kid."

Glimmer shook her fiery hair loose. She tossed her glasses into the water and pulled on her lucky green goggles. "I know you're aces with a plane, Clint Sparks, but this ain't no boat."

Sparks smiled and buckled his own seat belt. "Hold on kid. I have a hunch. Call it intuition."

Glimmer gritted her teeth. "Granny would call it idiocy."

Sparks cut off the banter and jammed the gear shift back into drive. He slammed his foot on the pedal and raced down the bank of the path and into the roaring water.

A wave of cascading liquid slammed into the windshield, some of it leaping over to splash them soaking wet. There was no time to turn back.

"Show some faith!" Sparks hollered.

Afi couldn't hear him, the roar was too deafening. She felt the truck begin to lose traction and she knew time was up.

"Bad idea, Sparks."

Sparks didn't answer. He gripped the wheel with white knuckles, battling the raging water as the vehicle surged forward. Soon they would be submerged. He was just about to tell Afi to bail out when a loud thunderous noise struck, and the pair felt the vehicle rattle as something clamped it.

"What the..."

Before he could finish, he felt the vehicle begin to lift. Whatever had grabbed hold of it now had full control. He let go of the wheel as the small truck slowly began to ascend out of the water yet still on a trajectory toward the heart of the waterfall.

Glimmer stared in amazement as she could see the vehicle's tires emerge from the water, and she finally saw that a huge metal clamp had locked itself around the wheel barrels. They were being drawn forward by a hydraulic lift.

"It's like driving through a car wash inside a convertible!" The energetic youth exclaimed.

Sparks was about to answer, but closed his lips tightly as they headed directly through the water. The journey only lasted a matter of seconds, but when it was over, he let out a breath of air, his face purple from holding it.

Glimmer was drenched. The sopping German uniform floating around her tiny hips, but she was no worse for wear. The vehicle finally came to a halt inside a darkly lit cavern.

"We made it!" Sparks whispered.

Glimmer looked around. A gust of hot air caused her nose to wrinkle. "Made it to where?"

✩ ✩ ✩

The water around them had drained completely as the vehicle had been lifted into a sealed compartment. Sparks and Glimmer realized they were actually inside the waterfall, having been directed to a man made cavern. The gigantic structure was well lit, and apparently soundproof, for they could no longer hear the powerful waterfall.

"They must be using the water as an energy source for electricity." Sparks marveled. "But why go through this elaborate charade? What the hell can they be hiding down here?"

It didn't take long for company to arrive. A half dozen Nazi troopers trotted out from steel doors. They all bared weapons.

"Nice work, Sparks!" Glimmer pouted.

The rowdy soldiers parted to allow a small procession to emerge from the doorway. Two meek looking lab assistants strode forward. They obstructed Sparks view.

"Who are you?" the American aviator demanded. "And where is Professor Thatcher?"

A tall, lanky figure slithered from behind the white jacketed men. This towering figure marched toward the dented truck at a slow gait.

Glimmer gasped. "Oh, boy!"

Her shock and horror were directed at the menacing man's face. Below his shiny bald head, he wore a monocle, but it was his visage that frightened the young girl. His face was scarred and purplish, as if he had suffered great burns.

"Only a face a mother could love," Sparks whispered, trying to calm his young ward.

Glimmer was still shaking. "My god, Sparks. He has a face that could peel wallpaper!"

The giant Nazi halted only a foot from the truck front end. He stood, feet apart, hands clasped behind his back.

"It is not often we get guests to this island," he said. His voice was a low grumble, as if he labored to speak.

Sparks began to rise from the driver's seat, but plunged back down quickly as pistols greeted him. "Easy boys. Let's not start an international incident."

The lanky man allowed himself a smile.

He waved a hand for the soldiers to lower their weapons.

"That's better." Sparks barked, with a hint of sarcasm.

The scarred man studied the pilot for a full half minute, and then turned his attention to the fiery red head.

"Stop staring at me Karloff!"

The German snorted. "American wit. I have seen the adaptation of Shelley's novel. Colin Clive was far more interesting a character than big old Boris. You see, little girl, without Doctors, there can be no heroes."

Glimmer edged away from the man, still fearful of his wretched features.

"What about John Thatcher?" She spit out, trying to show courage.

"And his daughter," Sparks added.

Again they were met with a moment of silence. The lanky man motioned for his guards to frisk the pair. The soldiers did so rather haphazardly as one of them made the mistake of searching Afi's hair. The angry Nazi paid for his transgression with an elbow to the midsection.

"Feisty! I like that," the leader acknowledged. "No wonder you picked up this native in your travels, although she's a bit too young for my taste."

Sparks bared his teeth. "It's not like that you dirty dog!"

The lanky German only snickered, reveling in his success at perturbing the American pilot.

"You American, always so defensive and hostile, completely opposite the cordial British. I fear you will be more of a hindrance than Her Majesty's finest."

Sparks was still seething. "I asked about Professor Thatcher."

"In good time, my man. Let me introduce myself. I'm Dieter Ferdinand, the curator of this domain."

Glimmer razed him. "One of Adolph's boys, I'm sure."

Ferdinand ignored the youth. "You are most certainly a Yankee," he barked at Sparks. "Why the interest in a British professor? Wait don't answer that. It can only be one thing. The one thing all of you greedy Americans strive for. Money."

Sparks didn't reply.

The German continued. "The British, themselves, must have hired you, for such an expedition is beyond their childish minds. They built the world's largest navy, content to sit back and bask in the glory of their achievement, while the rest of the world began to construct aerial weapons. It will be the downfall of the British empire."

"That sounds like a threat," Glimmer snarled, no longer so fearful of the man.

Dieter only turned and smiled at the youth. "You should not be ashamed of your heritage little girl. Coloring you hair and wearing ghoulish clothing cannot hide your features. Your inferiority rises above the disguise."

"Leave her out of this!" Sparks demanded. "Just tell me about Thatcher."

Dieter was nonchalant. "Your suspicions are correct. He is here. We are utilizing his research skills."

"Did he offer these skills freely or was he forced?" Sparks inquired, unsure of himself.

Dieter didn't answer.

"What do you intend to do with us?" Glimmer whispered.

The evil German merely shrugged. "I'm a scientist, my friend. If it were up to me..."

Sparks nodded. "But you're just following orders, right?"

Dieter flashed a grin. "I'm a soldier first."

Glimmer fought back sobs. "At least tell us what this is about."

Dieter ran a gloved hand down the girl's cheek. "I suppose it can't harm anyone. You see, young woman, there is a great war coming. We've known it for awhile now. The world is restless, and things must change. In order to create change, you must have a pecking order. Clearly, the Aryan race is at the top of the chain. Our superiority is evident at every level, knowlege, strength, even beauty."

Sparks spit on the cavern floor.

"Blah, blah, blah," he mocked. "Heard it before, and you should talk. Your mug would inspire Halloween masks, you creepy, old..."

Before he could finish, Dieter Ferdinand silenced him with a vicious slap across the face. A trickle of blood dripped down Sparks chin.

"Quiet, fool!" He paced back and forth, measuring himself. "There was a time, this young lady would have found me attractive, but I made a sacrifice for the fatherland. An experiment rendered me this way."

"You blew yourself up, genuis?" Afi laughed. "Must have been the superior mind."

Dieter raised his hand as if to strike her too, but snatched it back. "No, you will serve other purposes for our cause." He again stroked her cheek with a gloved hand.

Sparks could bear no more. He lunged for the doctor, only to be repelled by the butt of a steel pistol.

Dieter laughed. "Typical American bravado. All you lack is the white horse and ridiculous ten gallon hat your matinee cowboys wear."

He motioned for the guards to tie up the prisoners.

"So this is it, Clint," Afi whispered. "Granny will wonder what happened to us."

Sparks mustered up courage. "Maybe we'll be able to tell her ourselves."

✩ ✩ ✩

Bound with taut ropes, Clint Sparks and his aide, Glimmer, were transported down a brightly lit corridor, past several laboratories and finally into a darkened broom closet. They were shoved harshly inside by their captors. The bare room was lit sparsely by a single dim light bulb.

"Sparks, look!" Glimmer demanded, pointing at a limp form in the corner.

The American aviator rushed toward the slumping figure. In the pale light, he could barely make out that it was a human being he was advancing toward. The form was huddled, fetal like, under a grey blanket.

Sparks yanked back the natty cloth. Much to his shock, under the grime and soot, he recognized the features of a female.

"Miss Thatcher!" He gulped, shaking her roughly.

Glimmer gasped. The young female was disheveled, her chest still. "Is she dead?"

Sparks bent his head low on the girl's bosom. She was clad only in rags, most likely a potato sack. Her skin was cool to the touch, but he detected a feint heartbeat.

"She's alive!" He breathed out with relief.

Glimmer kneeled and began rubbing the girl's arms and legs, restoring circulation to the unconscious female. It was a laborious task for the strong willed Polynesian, her own hands still bound with rope.

Clint struggled with his own bonds, able to move his fingers dexterously toward his ankles where he was able to extract a sharp file he always kept inside his boots. With much effort, he was able to cut through his bonds and immediately released Afi as well.

"Sparks, those fiends! Look at this dame. She must be starving."

A dribble of spit formed on Kate Thatcher's lips as her eyelids fluttered with revival. The girl gazed wide eyed at Glimmer, fearfully.

"It's okay missy, we're the good guys," Afi spat out in a reassuring tone.

Kate Thatcher wiped a numb hand across her cracked lips. The soot from her face clouded her vision, and her nostrils were clogged with the nauseating odor of raw coal.

"Daddy?" she croaked weakly. She tried to rise from the floor, but her knees gave out and she plummeted roughly to the floor.

Sparks reached out instinctively, but the girl shrank from his touch.

"Please, don't!" she begged.

Afi grabbed her roughly by the shoulders. "There's no time for this, woman. Toughen up and fill us in on what's happening."

Kate Thatcher responded well to the chiding. Her trembling ceased and she was able to gain enough strength to lean against the cold wall.

"Tell us what happened to your father. You are John Thatcher's daughter, are you not?" Sparks prompted.

The young British girl crawled closer to the pair. Even covered with grime and weak from dehydration, her beauty was evident. She caught Sparks staring at her and tugged at her meager wardrobe modestly.

"My father and I were tricked by these evil men," she began. "We were led to believe this was a scientific expedition to study volcanic activity in this region, but the Germans had other plans."

Sparks nodded. "You refer to your father's expertise on coal?"

Thatcher nodded. "Yes, that horrible man, Ferdinand, at first he seemed so nice. He gave father and I everything we requested. All our demands were met and we couldn't believe our luck when they took us to this island. Daddy spotted the volcanic cones from the airplane. Many of them are active."

Glimmer grew restless. "What about the coal? What does baldy want with it?"

Thatcher shot her a look of incredulity. "Isn't it obvious? We're on an underdeveloped island in Malaysia. The German nationals are seeking to inhabit this island as a war base for their evil intentions. The only problem is getting around. The Japanese got here first, but they only have bicycles. The Nazis want to occupy the island with motor vehicles, and that's why they need my father."

"Fuel," Sparks muttered.

The attractive Brit smiled. 'Daddy is an expert on energy extraction. He has developed a method to extract a powerful octane source from the plentiful supply of coal."

"So they can fill up the tanks on their cars," Afi finished.

Thatcher nodded. "Not just that. It's worse. Ferdinand had his own ideas on the subject. With my father filling in the final missing equations, the pair were able to create a super fuel, capable of powering any automobile, motor boat or airplane."

Sparks eyes grew wide. "And it works?"

The beautiful British girl choked back a sob. Her throat was dry. "It will when the kinks are worked out. Daddy got suspicious of Ferdinand when he wouldn't let us leave to reveal our invention. It became apparent that the fuel was intended strictly for German conquest so daddy held back on some key ingredients."

"Meaning what?"

"Meaning that this so called super fuel is very volatile. Without expert supervision, it can create a chain reaction that would be disastrous."

Sparks grunted, his mind churning with deliberate intentions.

"Where is your father now, Miss Thatcher?"

The girl bit her lower lip. "I have not seen my father in over a week."

The trio were interrupted by the sudden opening of the door. In the frame of the doorway stood the monstrous form of Dieter Ferdinand, a sinister smile draped across his lips. His medical smock was covered with blotches of scarlet blood.

Kate Thatcher forced himself to rise from the cold floor. She pounded her tiny fists on the massive German's chest. Immediately, two soldiers pushed their way forward and shoved her viciously against the wall.

Sparks reacted instinctively. He looped an overhand right at the hostile soldier, landing a crushing blow against the man's temple. The Nazi stiffened before sagging limply to the ground. Sparks was immediately greeted with the cold end of a rifle against his chest, staggering him back.

"Please, Miss Thatcher, enough with your theatrics!" Dieter Ferdinand insisted.

The beautiful Brit only sobbed as she forced herself to snarl at him. "You fiend!"

Ferdinand shrugged haphazardly. "I'll admit your suspicions are correct. This is your father's blood, but don't despair, the old coot lives." The lanky German leered at her heaving bosom. "You see, we figured out that he had tried to trick us by leaving out the final ingredient in his recipe

...she pounded tiny fists on the German's massive chest...

for superfuel, so we had a little discussion." He wolfishly grinned and pointed at his blood smeared outfit.

"I hate you, you evil man!" The girl whispered.

Undeterred, Ferdinand continued. "Professor Thatcher refused to divulge the last part of the equation, even at risk of his well being, but then it dawned on me, I had a bigger bargaining chip."

Sparks shook his groggy head. "All you guys are the same, unwilling to do the hard work yourself. You'll never rule the world."

"That remains to be seen." The evil scientist turned to the sparsely clad female. "Perhaps your father's stubbornness will fade when it is your blood on my hands?"

Sparks lunged ferociously at the threat, but he was met with violent resistance.

Ferdinand laughed. "Bring the American too. Maybe his feistiness will subside after watching Miss Thatcher suffer, knowing his tiny exotic friend will meet the same fate."

Glimmer shook a fist at him. "Get lost Karloff! You don't scare me!"

Sparks swallowed hard. He admired his young ward's spunk, but he knew time was running out for them.

☆ ☆ ☆

The German outfit escorted the prisoners down the corridor into a small laboratory where a thin, malnourished, man slumped over on a workbench. It was John Thatcher. It was evident he had been brutally beaten by his captors. Sparks silently acknowledged the professor's bravery.

Kate Thatcher perked up upon seeing her father.

"Daddy, you're alive!"

Before the father and daughter could be reunited, Dieter Ferdinand blocked the reunion, flanked by two armed guards.

"Sadly, this heartwarming scene will be short lived, unless you surrender the missing formula, Professor Thatcher."

Kate Thatcher spat at the German scientist who obstructed her path.

"Don't listen to him, daddy! They intend to use the fuel for harm!"

John Thatcher curled his lips in defeat. "I would gladly have given my own life for Queen and country, but I cannot ask that of my only child. You win, you monster, I will give you the formula."

Dieter Ferdinand could not contain his elation. He whooped excitedly, "The Fuehrer will reward my achievement greatly."

Thatcher shrugged in defeat. "Yes, of course, well let's get it over with." He stalked back to his test tubes in sullen defeat, slowly mixing a few vials of liquid together. In mere seconds, he was finished.

"My good man, you have made the correct choice." Ferdinand proclaimed. "Now give it to me!"

Thatcher hesitated. Ferdinand snapped his fingers and instantly the Germans aimed their guns at the helpless daughter.

In that moment, John Thatcher's eyes lit with fire. Clint Sparks caught that expression, one that only a parent could understand.

"Here you go." Thatcher said nonchalantly as his wrists flicked unexpectedly, showering the two German guards with the contents of the vials.

The courageous Brit had made the decision long before the German party had entered his lab for the final time. He knew the treacherous Ferdinand would never agree to let them leave the island unharmed, so Thatcher had planned his moment in deliberation. He had cautiously filled the vials with deadly acid which now ravaged the faces of his abusers.

Clint Sparks had suspected this move and was prepared. He tackled the massive German scientist, even as his body guards screamed in agony.

One of the soldiers miraculously was able to fire off a round from his rifle before slumping to the ground, lifeless. The tiny confines of the lab made the roar of the gunfire thunderous. Sparks heard Kate Thatcher scream, and felt his heart drop, he couldn't turn his attention away from the German goliath, Dieter Ferdinand, who even now, was recovering from the aviator's rush.

"You dirty American!" Ferdinand, cursed, his thick fingers, gripping Sparks throat.

Sparks struggled vainly to break the chokehold. In his weakened form, he caught the drifting sound of chaos. Glimmer was shouting and yelling at the Thatchers, urging them to flee.

"Good girl," he thought, fighting against blacking out. "At least she'll get them to safety."

Dieter Ferdinand was on top of him now, reeling blow after blow against the weakened aviator. Sparks felt his wounds re-open as blood seeped into his eyes, blinding him. He was about to lose consciousness when he heard Afi's voice trilling.

"Get up flyboy! Granny's expecting us back home!" The youth demanded.

The encouraging sound of the girl's voice filled Sparks with a renewed vigor. He reached down into his well of energy for one last effort as he gripped the German's mighty wrists.

Ferdinand gritted his teeth and hung on tenaciously, but it was too late. A surge of strength flowed through Clint Spark's body, his hands clamping down hard on his foe. With a ferocious yell he yanked with all his might.

The resulting crack of Dieter Ferdinand's wrists left the massive German speechless. He yelped, his broken limbs dangling. He looked up in disbelief to see the fiery haired form of Glimmer leaning over him.

"Leave my father alone!" She snarled, smashing the butt of a rifle against the temple of the evil scientist. Ferdinand's eyes rolled back. He was out before his chin crashed against the cold floor.

Clint Sparks shook the cobwebs out of his head. One thought tore through his mind.

"Kate!" he yelled frantically searching for the beautiful Brit.

He expected to see her lifeless form, but instead he saw her cradling her father's head. The scientist was coughing, sputtering blood with each gasp. He had taken the blast from the German soldier squarely in the chest. It was obvious his life was forfeit.

"Kate, we have to go," he whispered softly.

The girl said nothing, numb from feeling. Afi gently offered her a hand as Sparks raced to the lab table. He filled up a beaker with the super fuel.

"Sparks, are you crazy?" Glimmer asked. "That stuff is unstable."

The wounded aviator sighed. "It's the only way we can get off this island!"

✩ ✩ ✩

Fearful that other Germans may be lurking around the laboratory, Clint Sparks ordered Glimmer to take Kate Thatcher topside and wait for his escape. The youth protested vainly, but did not challenge his stern orders. Sparks only wanted to shelter the girls from the horrific death scene.

Stealthily, he worked, dousing the laboratory and the surrounding offices with fuel as he made his way back to the hydraulic lift. His intentions were obvious. He meant to blow the lab up, removing any evidence of its existence. If anyone questioned the explosion, he would blame it on volcanic activity.

The truck was gone. Afi and Kate Thatcher had made it out safely. Only problem was, Clint Sparks would be unprotected by the safe interior the motor vehicle provided. He would have to risk his weakened body against the unforgiving waterfall!

With a lunatic howl, he activated the sensor that operated the lift and with a dexterous flip tossed a wooden match down into the trail of superfuel he had left below. A whoosh of flame sparked momentarily, but Sparks was already in the lift, holding on for dear life as water cascaded around him. Even with the thunderous pressure of the waterfall deafening him, he could hear massive explosions echoing from the laboratory below.

He grinned wolfishly as the raging waters tossed him blindly into the current. He felt his nostrils fill up and his body twisted and turned raggedly in the churning water. The pain was a dull ache as his body was already numb from the water pressure. He felt drained as he sought valiantly to claw his way up from the bubbling pool.

It seemed and eternity before his hand reached air, and then the rest of his weary limbs emerged from the shallow depths. He held his nose and blew, desperately to pop his ears.

"About time old man!"

He vaguely registered the young Polynesian's sarcastic voice as she dragged him out collar first. Kate Thatcher stood dripping wet off to the side, her torn rags clinging to her voluptuous body. Sparks momentarily felt a sense of shame at his thoughts, but shrugged it off. The girl was beautiful, even in her rugged shape.

"Glimmer, is there enough gas in that German truck to make it back to the Blackburn?"

Afi registered a deep look of concentration before shrugging. "Does it matter?"

Sparks drove the commandeered vehicle as recklessly as he dared through the deep jungle path, occasionally frightening a nest of monkeys from their casual dining. He was so intent on getting away from the massive cloud of smoke and fire they had left behind at the laboratory that he didn't see the Japanese infantry men in the road ahead of them.

Fortunately, Glimmer still wore her lucky green goggles, and they aided her in spotting the treacherous bike riders.

"Sparks! Nips at twelve o'clock!" She barked.

Clint Sparks tugged at the shivering form of Kate Thatcher who rode shotgun. No time for gentleness. He yanked her fragile body down roughly to the seat of the truck. Glimmer stood in back, both hands gripping the safety bar. They were going too fast for her to try and attempt a shot.

"Oh crap!" She hollered holding on for dear life.

The tired aviator mumbled for her to tie a belt to the safety bar, but he never looked back. His concentration was fully on the pint sized menaces standing between him and freedom.

The Japanese men casually pulled aside for the German vehicle, fully cooperating with their newly formed partners. It was with utter surprise when they noticed Sparks' audaciousness.

The infantrymen screamed curses and insults before unloading a stream of gunfire at the truck, but their aim proved futile as Sparks held his foot to the pedal, leaving them behind frustrated and confused.

In all the wildness of the moment, he had forgotten the humble Kate Thatcher, her head inches from his thigh. The girl pulled away with a semblance of dignity.

"What was that horrible noise back there?" She croaked, barely audible.

"I covered our tracks." Sparks answered. "There will be nothing for any curious eyes to find."

The beautiful blonde choked a sob, "Poor Daddy."

Clint patted her shoulder affectionately. "He died a hero. He saved all our lives."

"We never should have come to this wretched island. All Daddy wanted was to make the world more energy efficient."

Sparks nodded uncomfortably. "We have to get you out of here safely so his sacrifice will not have been in vain." He cleared his sore throat. "How you making out back there?"

Glimmer didn't answer. A chill shot down the aviator's spine. He spun wildly in the seat. "Afi!"

The fiery red head was slumped over the bar, her hands covered in scarlet. She had been wounded in their escape!

☆ ☆ ☆

Sparks started to take his foot off the gas pedal, but a firm hand gripped his shoulder. He turned to see Kate Thatcher staring at him. Her blue eyes beamed with determination and vigor.

"Keep driving!" She growled. "I have medical training. I'll look after the girl."

Sparks decided to forego his reaction to ease up. He mashed a foot down hard on the pedal.

"Please, she's everything to me!"

Kate Thatcher didn't answer. She was busy ripping strips off her already torn remnants of clothing in a valiant effort to stem the blood loss.

"Go faster, Yank!" She barked.

Sparks allowed himself a moment to register a gaze at the fuel gauge. As if things couldn't get worst, the needle hovered dangerously close to empty. He made a daring decision to go off road and race the beach dunes. A truck was meant to be ridden hard like a stallion. He could hear only Kate Thatcher's labored breathing from the back. Afi remained silent.

☆ ☆ ☆

The vehicle tore across the dunes at a breath neck pace, jolting Sparks from his seat on several occasions. On one such occasion, he heard Glimmer moan in agony. Never in his wildest dreams, could he have imagined gaining so much joy from the girl's agony.

"She's alive!" He proclaimed with zealous vigor.

Kate Thatcher continued to work on the poor girl. Despite her own weakness, the British youth maintained a steady hand as she battled to save the young ward of Clint Sparks.

The beefy aviator allowed himself a brief glimpse back. Thatcher's clothing hung barely above her kneecaps, torn and shredded for medical bandages. Even covered in grime and soot, he could see her limbs were enticing. He allowed himself to imagine her in an evening gown, dancing under the stars with him.

His reverie was interrupted by a sputtering and conking of the truck engine.

"No! Damn it!" He lamented. The needle of the gas gauge had dipped below red. They were bone dry. The engine had sucked up every last drop. "Please for the love of God just a few more moments. I can't lose this child!"

He slammed his fists on the steering wheel in torment.

"Sparks, look!" Kate Thatcher prompted.

Over the next dune, they could see the flipper of his Blackburn shark.

"My ship!" Sparks roared. "We made it!"

☆ ☆ ☆

The Blackburn stood shimmering under the glaring heat. Apparently, the windy weather had blown its tarp away. Unfortunately, this action also allowed the nose of the bird to fill with sand.

Sparks prayed it hadn't gotten into the engines or propellers.

"Are you strong enough to get Afi into the aircraft?" He asked Kate Thatcher.

The suddenly energetic Brit ignored his question, instead focusing on his plane's decrepit shape. "The window has been smashed! How will you be able to drive this scrap of junk?"

There was a renewed feistiness in her voice. Sparks smiled back meekly. He had no answer for the girl.

His meditation was broken up by the thunderous booms off in the distance.

"Miss Thatcher, just how volatile was your father's formula?"

The girl gulped, wild eyed. "Daddy didn't say. He just said it was way too dangerous to test it on Great Britain's soil. That's the primary reason we took up Dieter Ferdinand's offer. "

Sparks felt the tremors through the sand. It was obvious the explosions had set off some sort of chain reaction.

"We can't wait this out! Get Afi in the ship and strap down."

The girl's eyes opened frightfully. "Don't tell me you're actually contemplating using that fuel to power our ride?" She didn't wait for his answer as a rumble underneath her feet tossed her roughly on her keister.

Sparks yanked her from the vehicle. "Get my daughter aboard now!"

Kate Thatcher didn't answer. She was already dragging the unconscious Polynesian aboard.

Sparks didn't hesitate. He emptied the contents of the beaker into his plane's fuel tank. He took one last look at the Flaming Pineapple logo before climbing aboard.

"Heaven help us, Granny will have my hide!"

☆ ☆ ☆

Luck was on their side as the mighty engines came to life and the familiar hum of the ship filled his ears. Afi had been strapped down in Smugglers bay, next to Big Guy. Kate Thatcher rode shotgun. Sparks had ripped a spare parachute apart to create a makeshift windshield. It wouldn't matter, he intended to fly low. The beaker's contents were equivalent to a drop of water in the desert.

If the British naval craft had moved even a bit since his adventure, they would plunge helplessly into the ocean!

Sparks had never attempted a lift off from a beach setting. The heavy Blackburn needed the sleek pavement to gather enough steam to propel upward for flight. The only saving grace was that the beach extended as far as the eye could see.

"Hold on woman!" He bellowed as he roared straight ahead.

Kate Thatcher tugged at her seatbelt before erupting in a maniacal laugh.

"What the hell are you clamoring about?" Sparks demanded.

The beautiful Brit continued her shrieking. "Don't you see how funny this is? I'm worried about a seat belt?"

Sparks took a moment before his nerves untangled and he too, let loose with guffaws. Much to his chagrin, a weakened Glimmer mumbled from the back.

"Stop playing Sparks and get this bird in the sky before this island blows!"

Sparks was so thrilled to hear the familiar taunts of his ward that he had forgotten that the superfuel explosion back at the lab had somehow ignited a dormant volcano.

"Well at least part of my explanation will be true!" He shouted, mainly to himself.

He was grateful for the diversion, the British girl's theatrics had provided. His knuckles were white from the death grip he had on the wheel but he felt the joyful sensation of being airborne.

"We have lift off!" He declared victoriously.

The moment had come none too soon. Sparks glanced down to his left as the massive aircraft ascended. The island was a great ball of fire in the area they had just occupied. The fiery flames had scorched the dense jungle and were threatening to head toward the beach.

As soon as the ship was stable, Kate Thatcher resumed her role as medic. She worked deftly to make Glimmer comfortable. Much to her happiness she had discovered the bullet had only grazed the child, resulting in tremendous blood loss, but thankfully no permanent damage.

Sparks was thrilled, congratulating himself for handling the affair so well. Unfortunately, his celebration was cut short as the plane began to rock heavily.

"Damn it!" He cursed. "Stupid, cocky, man."

"What's wrong?" Kate Thatcher inquired.

Sparks didn't want to alert the females. The superfuel was indeed not perfected. His instruments were reading wildly frantic. He had no way of knowing if they were off course as they roared across the blue seas.

"It's nothing," he declared in a monotone voice, hoping to mask his nerves. "Just hoping your man Harry lives up to his promise and has that aircraft carrier ready to cradle my baby Blackburn."

Thatcher ignored his mutterings, concentrating on making Afi comfortable. The young Polynesian had lifted her goggles to the top of her head. Her vision was blurred from weakness, but she had just enough oomph to thrust her body to a seated position.

"Don't get all cozy sister!" She ordered.

"I beg your pardon?" Thatcher retorted, thickening her accent.

Glimmer lifted a finger toward the cockpit. "That chair is mine once this gets over with."

"Whatever are you ranting about you silly little girl?" Kate Thatcher scolded. "It's a preposterous thought to even suggest I'd deign to ride in this god forsaken rust bucket ever again."

Sparks interjected, "No need to get personal, Miss Thatcher. The Flaming Pineapple may not have the shiniest visage you've ever feasted your spoiled eyes upon, but she's got a lot of good old fashioned grit in her sails."

"Are you both daft?" Kate Thatcher demanded. "Are all you Americans so insane?"

Strangely, Afi took that insult as a compliment. "Crazy enough to help the rest of the world out." She relaxed her body and patted Big Guy for luck. "Anyway, sister I'm sorry about your father. He really stepped up back there."

'So did his daughter," Sparks interjected.

Glimmer nodded humbly. "Thank you Miss Thatcher. I can see why flyboy has the giggles for you."

Thatcher wrinkled her nose, struggling with Afi's slang, but she had caught the gist of it.

"I'm honored to be rescued in this fine aircraft," she said with a straight face.

Sparks started to laugh, but his actions were interrupted by a massive altitude drop.

"Turbulance?" Afi wondered aloud.

Clint Sparks didn't answer. He knew the skies were calm. The superfuel was not reacting to the proper combustion. It was eating savagely against the Blackburn's engines.

"I'm afraid I have to confess this might not end well." Sparks admitted in defeat.

Kate Thatcher rolled her eyes incredulously. "The great Yankee flier, Clint Sparks, unable to steer this fine vessel to safety? Unacceptable!

Where did the British intelligence ever get off on the novelty that you could handle this mission?"

Sparks shrugged, he felt the plane bucking beneath him. He could see Glimmer grip the bottom of Big Guy fearfully.

Kate Thatcher refused to give in to her own fright. Instead she raced to the front of the plane and tore a bigger hole in the parachute material.

"How do you very well expect to spot an aircraft carrier with this bloody sheet blocking your vision?" She remarked.

Sparks didn't stop her. It didn't matter at this point. He knew the engine would seize any moment now, the propellers grinding to a halt and then it would be over in seconds.

"If we had more time..."

"Stop right there." Kate Thatcher commanded. "Look, down below!"

Sparks heart skipped a beat. Before them lay the magnificent aircraft carrier Harry Staish had promised. Vigor jolted him to grit his teeth.

"Hold on people this will be fun."

Kate Thatcher gripped his shoulder gently. "What was that about more time?" Her voice was soft, in earnest.

Clint Sparks gripped her delicate hands romantically. "When this is over and I get this bird repaired and my little girl patched up, maybe we could get together for a cup of coffee?"

"Coffee?" she mused. "Utterly revolting. We prefer a more civilized taste."

"Like a spot of tea?" Afi chimed in.

Sparks and Thatcher turned and joined in with the affable girl's chuckling. Despite the grinding of the ships engines and the sputtering of her propellers, Clint Sparks felt himself in total control.

"Maybe I can interest her in some of Granny's award winning ice tea?" Sparks proclaimed.

"Iced tea?" Thatcher retorted "Preposterous!"

The trio continued to banter as the aviator ace pointed his wounded bird to safety. His was a confident pose. Even as the propeller ceased churning and the plane plummeted toward the deck of the aircraft carrier, American, Clint "Solution" Sparks never doubted the outcome.

THE END

Remembering Terry & the Pirates

The genesis of my characters, Sparks and Glimmer, stems from my childhood obsession with comic strip characters. While everyone recognizes Dick Tracy, Flash Gordon and the Phantom, most of the younger generation have no clue about Milton Caniff's groundbreaking strip, Terry and the Pirates.

Unfortunately, the passage of time has dulled the impact of this creator's work. True comic art fans know Caniff as "The Rembrandt of Comics." His artwork and storytelling have inspired a list of modern illustrators too long to list here. Suffice to say, the man was a legend in his own time, once gracing the cover of Time magazine. He would author the adventures of Terry and the Pirates for a dozen years before departing in an unprecedented move to originate one of the first creator owned strips in history, Steve Canyon. This was monumental news back in the days.

How does this relate to my tale? Simple, it's a homage to the main characters from that classic strip, Pat Ryan and Terry Lee. Like those two fantastic adventurers, Solution Sparks and his young companion, Glimmer, travel throughout Asia seeking thrills and righting wrongs. I highly recommend readers seek out examples of Caniff's strip. I guarantee you will be hooked immediately.

I had tremendous fun writing this tale of aviation adventure and I hope it's just the beginning of the adventures of Solution Sparks.

ROBERT RICCI—is the author of Blood on the Cobblestones. He graduated from of Curry College, class of 1986 and is a lifelong resident of New England who grew up on a steady diet of Doc Savage novels, classic comic strips like Terry and the Pirates, etc. He loves the classic heroes, Flash Gordon, Tarzan, Conan and all the rest. He's also a huge fan of 1960s television series. Last but not least, he's the proud father of two adult young ladies and lives a quiet life with his better half, Dorothy.

Operation Blow-Up

Fred Adams, Jr.

4 July 1943, Overton, Kansas

The heat was oppressive, but the Colonel didn't want the windows down because of the dust, so Corporal Logan turned the car's fan up full blast and wiped the sweat that pooled under his eyes every minute or two. Overton, Kansas, population 835, according to the sign he just passed. Two or three more miles, and they should reach their destination.

The car was standard Army issue: a humpbacked '41 Ford sedan, olive drab with a star and numbers stenciled on either front door, identifying the car as government property. As if somebody would steal a car this ugly, Logan thought, even for a joyride.

He looked in the rearview mirror. The Colonel's eyes were closed. He was taking a nap. Rank has its privileges, he thought. Logan was waiting at the airfield when the Colonel arrived, and he was the only passenger on the airplane. No adjutant, no underling to fetch and do his bidding, no WAC secretary to keep him amused in his off hours. Logan's orders were simple: Do what the Colonel tells you, and keep your mouth shut.

The Colonel was all business. He returned Logan's salute, handed him a slip of paper with their destination, and climbed into the back seat of the Ford without waiting for Logan to open the door. In less than a minute, they were kicking up Kansas dust.

The sun beat down on the Ford, blazing through the windows and turning the car into a rolling greenhouse. When Logan began to roll down his window, the Colonel said one of the few things he would say to the Corporal all day, "Leave it up."

Logan drove through the gate of the Monroe County Fairground under a banner that proclaimed: Monahan's Aviation Spectacle - featuring the Flying Daredevils. The parking area, little more than a pasture, was crowded with rattletrap cars and farm trucks. All had one thing in common, a layer of dust that turned them all the same dun hue under the blue bowl of the sky.

"Over there, Corporal." The Colonel pointed to a Ford sedan, identical except for the paint job with two men standing beside it. A government car and government men. The pair wore suits, jackets and all, and hats in the heat. Logan had been around enough to understand they kept them on to hide the holsters underneath.

Logan stopped the car, and the Colonel climbed out of the back seat without waiting for Logan, who clambered out of the driver's seat, embarrassed that he was slow in his attendance.

"Wait here." Logan would remember two things about the Colonel from that afternoon: one, the scar that ran from his right ear to his upper lip, and the other the coldness of the stare from his slate grey eyes. Logan saluted, and the Colonel walked away to join the agents.

"Welcome to Podunk, Colonel," jibed one of the men. Collins was his name. "Where's our boy?"

Jennings, Collins' partner, made a sweeping gesture with his arm. "Right this way, sir."

The fairground arena was little more than a level field with sets of wooden bleachers lining either side. A dirt oval ringed the grassy center, a quarter-mile track for trotter races. The bleachers were filled with noisy people of every age and description, men in overalls, men in suits, women in gingham dresses, and barefoot children.

Overhead, an airplane engine droned. The plane was just a speck in the sky, but the Colonel's trained eye immediately recognized it as a Curtiss Jenny, probably one of the biplanes auctioned off at the end of World War I. As it got closer, he could see the plane was painted with red and white stripes and a field of white stars on blue on the wings.

A voice crackled over a tinny public address system. "Ladies and Gentlemen, Monahan's Aviation Spectacle is proud to present our main attraction. You've seen him earlier with the Flying Daredevils, and now here he is to show you what he can do flying solo, the Flying Phenomenon, the amazing Billy Chadwell." On the field, a man in coveralls and a leather cap waved a green flag the size of a pillowcase, good to go.

The crowd cheered, but Billy Chadwell couldn't hear it over the snarl of the Jenny's engine as he swooped over the treetops and shot past the grandstands of the Monroe County Fairground, his blue scarf trailing six feet behind him in the wind. Billy pulled back on the stick and the plane climbed just enough for the landing gear to brush the tops of the pines at the end of the field and set them waving. He knew the closer he came to disaster, the louder the crowd would cheer.

An outside loop over the endless fields of corn beside the arena, then another fly-by. The wind sock that hung from the flagpole below Old Glory was limp. Perfect weather for what Billy liked to call a day at the office. On the ground, he saw Cap Monahan, owner and operator of Monahan's Aviation Spectacle, an inch tall from the sky, waving the green flag, his signal that the arena was clear for Billy's next stunt.

He nosed the plane down, just enough to give him clearance for a barrel roll. To his left at about a forty-five degree angle, Billy spotted the water tank he had seen earlier and decided to use as a reference point. It was probably the tallest thing within twenty miles.

Billy corrected his course, putting the tank between the nose of the plane and the wingtip. He eased back on the stick, and as soon as he saw the nose of the plane clear the horizon, he eased the stick left. The Jenny tilted and Billy kept a firm hand on the controls, holding the nose of the plane forty-five degrees off the water tank, tracing a circle around it with the nose.

Ninety degrees; the wings were perpendicular to the ground, but Billy wasn't watching the ground. He was watching the tank to keep the Jenny's nose at that same forty-five degree angle as he rolled the plane over and upright again. What Billy saw was the horizon spinning around the tank. What the crowd saw was an airplane flying a corkscrew path.

The Colonel stood impassive as the crowd roared its approval.

"And now, folks, hold your breath, because Billy Chadwell, the Flying Phenomenon is going to do not one, not two, but three somersaults in mid-air. He doesn't wear a parachute, ladies and gentlemen, because he'd have no time to open it before he hits terra firma."

Two hands rolled a wheeled platform onto the center of the field. A bull's eye target was painted on a two-foot wooden disc and mounted on a two-by-four. Its center was five feet in the air.

"On the third loop, Billy will attempt the most daring stunt of the day. He will swoop down and hit the target you see in the center of the arena, not five feet off the ground at over a hundred miles an hour, and pull out of his dive just in time to avoid calamity."

Monahan was holding up a yellow caution flag. Overhead, Billy was looping around the arena and climbing for the right altitude.

"This stunt requires absolute concentration for Billy to succeed. We must ask, ladies and gentlemen, that no one move during the execution of this incredible maneuver." His voice rose in volume and pitch. "And now, Billy Chadwell, the Flying Phenomenon in the triple target loop!"

Monahan waved the green flag, and Billy set his path. He worked the stick forward and the Jenny began its dive. The angle was sharp, and the spectators were certain that he was going to bury his prop in the field.

Billy watched the ground as it came closer and closer. He watched the target as his reference mark, then at the last second, he pulled back on the stick, and the Jenny snarled in a tight curve between the grandstands and curved upward in a graceful climb. At the top of the arc, the Jenny continued its path and began its second dive. This one cut a little bit closer, and Billy could imagine the gasps from the audience. He finished the second loop time and went into the third. At the top of the arc, Billy said under his breath to the Jenny, "As you love me, darlin'."

The stunt was perilous enough doing three loops. There was always the possibility of a blackout, but adding the target made the stunt doubly dangerous. He had to hit the target with his landing gear at the very bottom of the dive while keeping the prop clear and still allow time to clear the trees. His timing had to be perfect. He went into the final dive, air whistling past his helmet, and his scarf trailing straight out behind him.

Billy pulled the stick back and the sharp curve of the dive softened. His landing gear hung twenty feet off the hard-packed soil of the arena. Ten feet. Five. The wheels straddled the target and the axle caught it dead center. Billy pulled back on the stick and the Jenny glided effortlessly over the tops of the pines.

The crowd that had been holding its breath let it out in one great shout.

"How about that, ladies and gentlemen? Let's hear it for the Flying Phenomenon, Billy Chadwell."

Billy did a Cuban eight and swooped down over the arena for the finale. He pulled a cable that released a cloud of smoke from the rear of the plane, and he soared over the arena, doing a double barrel roll and drawing a white corkscrew in the sky. "The Stars and Stripes Forever" blared from the p. a. system.

The Colonel turned to Collins and Jennings. "Bring him to me when he lands."

Billy landed the Jenny in the center of the field and taxied to stop beside the target. He shut down the engine, and pushed back his goggles. The world became a blur for a few seconds, until he hooked his eyeglasses over his ears and peered through their thick lenses. His goggles had lenses ground to his prescription.

He climbed out of the cockpit and was immediately surrounded by the crowd, people wanting to shake his hand, or to ask him to autograph his picture in the program book the air show peddled for a dime. He was signing one for a pretty brunette when he saw the two men in suits pushing to the front of the crowd.

"Mister Chadwell," the taller one said. "We're going to have to ask you to come with us." He flashed a badge too quickly for Billy to read the words on it.

"What's this all about?" Billy was racking his mind trying to think of anything he'd done that was remotely illegal.

"Just come with us, Mister Chadwell," the shorter one said, taking him by the elbow.

The crowd groaned in protest. Monahan started over, a startled look on his face. "Where you taking him?"

The tall agent left Billy's side and collared Cap. He spoke to him in low tones, and Cap backed off. "It's okay, folks," Billy said with a grin. "Stick around. I'll be right back," although he suspected that he wouldn't.

They led Billy to an olive green Ford with military markings. A corporal opened the door for him and said, "Inside."

Billy climbed into the back seat of the car and sat beside a tall man in Army pink and green, dark green over khaki, a full colonel. Billy noticed the scar on his face and wondered why the Colonel had no ribbons on his chest to hint at what theater of operations gave it to him.

The inside of the car was hot, and the air was close. He began to sweat almost as soon as he sat down.

"Mister Chadwell, I am Colonel Reynald Hennessey. Raise your right hand. You are about to join the United States Army."

"But I'm 4-F, my eyesight—"

"I don't need your eyesight, Mister Chadwell, I need your considerable skill in spite of it. Raise your right hand."

In less than a minute, Billy Chadwell, citizen became Billy Chadwell, Army Aviator.

"I'm certain that I don't need to explain the term 'top secret' to you, do I?"

"No, sir, I understand."

"We have an operative trapped in occupied France, and it is imperative that we get him out of there. You will fly him out."

"Excuse me, sir, but don't you have plenty of pilots over there already?"

"None that are so perfectly suited for this mission as you. We could train someone to do the things I've seen you do today, but we have no time. We have to perform the extraction within the next four days."

"Well, how will I get there?" Billy stammered. "Will there be a plane there for me to use?"

"We will fly you there. You will take your airplane with you."

"I don't get it."

"All in good time, Mister Chadwell. It will all become clear very soon."

The corporal, whose name Billy learned was Logan, drove them to the next county where an emergency landing field lay amid hundreds of acres of wheat. The orange and white checkerboard of the tower and the shed glowed in the afternoon sun. A Douglas C-47 was parked at the far end of the runway.

"Who all's going on the Skytrain?" Billy said.

Hennessey, who had been looking out the window at the monochrome landscape turned and said, "You and I."

"That's it?"

Hennessey didn't answer. Instead, he told Logan, "Pull up beside the plane."

As they approached, two men in pilot's gear came out of the checkered utility shed. Logan stopped the car, and once again was too slow to open Hennesey's door for him. The pilots snapped to attention and saluted. "We're fueled and ready, Colonel," Wilcox, the ranking pilot told him.

"We'll take off immediately, then. We should make Harper by morning." He pointed to Billy. "This is Lieutenant Chadwell. He'll be coming with us. See that he's comfortable."

That was a cruel joke. The inside of the Skytrain was a long tube with metal seats welded to the inside walls. Billy strapped himself into a seat over the wing where the turbulence would likely be the least. The Navigator was man named Perry, and a little guy named Baldwin manned the radio. The co-pilot, whose name was Barnes, brought him a parachute. "Stow this under the seat. Wilcox and I haven't cracked up yet, but there's always a first time."

Billy nodded grimly. "That's why they call C-47's 'flying coffins.'"

At an average airspeed of two hundred miles per hour, the C-47 made the trip west in fourteen hours with one stop to refuel. Billy decided that those were the most miserable hours he'd ever spent, strapped to the thinly upholstered metal seat and listening to the incessant drone of the engines echoing through the hollow body of the aircraft. He would doze off only to be jolted awake when the Skytrain hit turbulence. Once they flew through a thunderstorm, and the boom of thunder shook the plane like it was being shelled.

Billy still didn't know exactly what he was going to do. Hennessey couldn't discuss it in the car with Logan present, and he wouldn't discuss it in the airplane in spite of the noise to cover the sound of a conversation. I guess this is what 'top secret' really means, Billy thought.

It was dark when the plane landed, but Billy had a good idea where he was. As soon as his feet hit the ground, he heard the crunch of hard, alkalaine sand. He knew the plane was flying west by the sun, and estimating air speed versus overland distance, he was guessing California or northern Arizona, or maybe that corner where the two states butted against Nevada.

The runway lights had gone out as soon as the plane touched down, and the field was in near total darkness. A Jeep pulled up beside the plane, and he and Hennessey got in it. The headlights showed him the quonset hut shapes of hangars, a dozen or more, and finally a square, brick building, a barracks.

"Welcome to Harper Dry Lake Airfield, Lieutenant. Come with me." Hennessey led Billy inside where a sergeant behind a desk stood and saluted. He wore a name tag that read Smith. "Sergeant, make the Lieutenant comfortable."

This time comfort was no joke. The sergeant led Billy to a second-floor room that looked like a suite at a fancy hotel, a world away from the flea bags he stayed in touring with the air show. The room had a private bath and a real bed, not an Army field cot. The blackout curtains on the window looked as if they had come from Macy's.

"Would you like something to eat, Lieutenant?" Smith stood in the doorway, waiting to be dismissed.

"Sure, if it's no trouble."

"I'll have something sent up. Will there be anything else?"

"No, thanks." The sergeant was still waiting. "Uh, you can go."

"Just for your information, sir, the word is 'dismissed.'"

Billy decided that it would take a while for him to get used to being called "sir" and to giving orders.

In ten minutes, a corporal returned with a tray. Breakfast included ham and eggs, cottage fries, and coffee. He was ravenous and would have enjoyed every bite even if it weren't delicious. He'd heard veterans complain about Army food, but apparently this was an exception.

There was a knock at the door. It was Smith again with khakis over his arm and a Dopp kit in his hand. "For you, sir."

Billy unfolded the khakis. Lieutenant's bars were pinned to the blouse and the name tag read Jones. Remembering that Hennessey didn't use his name when he brought him into the barracks, the name tag made sense. Nobody's real name. Top secret.

He hung the uniform in the clothes press and stretched out on the bed. Whatever he had to worry about could wait until morning, which, judging by the Big Ben alarm clock on the night stand would arrive in about three hours. He was asleep in seconds.

☆☆☆

A Jeep pulled up beside the plane…

The jangling bell of the alarm clock woke Billy from a deep and dreamless slumber. He hadn't set the clock himself, but someone had. The room was pitch dark. Even if the sun were up, the curtains would block the light. He groped for his glasses on the night stand and switched on the lamp. Six a.m.

The alarm meant he was supposed to get up and get dressed. The water in the shower was hot; another step up from his usual accommodations, and a fresh blade in the Dopp kit's Gillette safety razor gave him a good clean shave. He was buttoning the khaki blouse when someone knocked on the door. It was a different sergeant with the same name tag, Smith. "If you are ready, would you come with me, sir?"

The sergeant led Billy downstairs to a mess hall. The windows were uncovered, and brilliant sunshine flooded the room. Thirty or so men were eating breakfast at tables. Some of the men, the ones with the G.I. haircuts were laughing, joking and conversing in an ordinary way. Men like himself, sporting odd hairstyles over their khakis sat either in silence, or in hushed head-to-head conversations. Their name tags said Jones, too.

Billy got a tray and went through the chow line. Breakfast was a reprise of the night before. He instinctively took a seat at one of the Smith tables, thinking he'd fit in better.

"Hi, guys."

The G.I.s looked up from their food and grunted a greeting, still shoveling in chow. One of them, a jug-eared fellow with sandy hair, said, "I'm Bob, this is Tom, and the dumb one at the end of the table is Roy."

"My name's Billy Chad-"

Bob held up his hand and pointed to the name tag. "Jones. Your name is Billy Jones." A statement, not a question. Billy caught on right away. No last names on anybody.

"Yep, Billy Chad Jones."

Conversation ranged from the Washington Senators' chances for a pennant win to which starlet was the sexiest pin-up to which Marx Brothers movie was funnier, *Duck Soup*, or *Night at the Opera*. Billy noticed that nobody talked about work or back home.

On his second cup of coffee, Billy saw Hennessey now in khakis standing in the doorway. He gave Billy a come-along gesture with his fingers. Billy turned in his tray and headed for the door.

Outside, the sun blazed on white sand and already made things in the distance dance in the heat. A groomed runway was lined with the hangars Billy saw the night before.

"Exactly what is this place, Colonel?"

"Harper Dry Lake Airfield is a government test site for experimental aircraft. I'm sure I don't have to remind you that everything you see here is top secret and not to be discussed on the outside."

They passed an open hangar and inside it Billy saw an airplane that instead of traditional projecting wings had a disc like a steel dish, its diameter almost the length of the fuselage, mounted to it by a spidery frame of steel brackets.

"That's the Nemuth Parasol," Hennessey said. "It was designed by students at Miami University to prove a circular wing would work as well as ordinary ones. The engineers here are exhaustively studying it for combat viability."

"I never heard of it."

"You wouldn't have. The military and intelligence communities exhaust every possible use for any new technology before the public is allowed to even know it exists."

Two hangars down the runway, they passed another open door where mechanics in coveralls were working on a plane that had not a circular wing, but an integrated circular wing and body with a pair of props mounted on either side of the cockpit and a pair of rounded tails at the rear. Billy stopped to stare at the odd aircraft.

"That's a prototype designed by Vought. They call it the 'Flying Pancake.' It's designed for short distance takeoff from a carrier, and it also takes up less space on deck. Believe it or not, Charles Lindbergh flew it once and said it was 'surprisingly easy to handle.'"

The door to the next hangar was closed. "Your plane is in here." Hennessey rapped on the hangar door and in a moment. it rolled upward. "Bring it out, Gus."

A man in coveralls rolled out something that looked like a wheelbarrow loaded with a steamer trunk under a tarp and topped with a small motor and propeller. He set it down in the open space in front of the hangar.

"There, Lieutenant, is your aircraft."

Billy walked around the mass, kicked it with his toe. "I don't get it."

"You will. Pay attention. You'll be doing this yourself before the day is over."

The mechanic unbuckled straps and undid catches, and what looked to be a tarp unfolded to spread on the ground in the shape of a flattened fuselage and wings. To Billy it looked like a fallen bird man. A second mechanic rolled out a gasoline-powered air compressor and pulled the starter cord. It chugged into life, and as Billy watched, air filled the shape, and over the course of ten minutes, it swelled from two dimensions to three, in the shape of a small airplane only four feet tall.

The wings were narrow, the nose boxy, and the fuselage a lean tapered tube ending in an oversized tail. The whole works was inner tube grey. The motor and prop were centered over the wings behind an open two-seat compartment. Billy looked inside and saw a full set of controls, stick and pedals, and a compact instrument panel. GA-33 was stenciled on the fuselage.

"Eight pounds of pressure per square inch," Gus said with a hint of pride. "Less than an auto tire, but you could stand on the wing if you weren't worried about tipping her over."

Billy poked at the wing with his forefinger. "What's she made of?"

"Goodyear calls it Airmat, a double layer of rubber coated nylon." He pointed to the engine. "Forty Horse McCullough engine'll take her to about fifty-two knots air speed."

"Sixty miles per hour," Billy said. "Not bad."

"Give or take. Climb rate is in the five hundred feet per minute ballpark. Flight range is around 275 miles."

"What's the ceiling?"

"Sixty-five hundred feet. I wouldn't take that high unless absolutely necessary. The air in the compartments expands at higher altitude. If you must, though, there's a bleeder valve to let off some of the pressure. A small compressor attached to the engine can restore the pressure at a lower altitude."

"What's the landing speed?"

"Thirty knots."

"Any more questions, Lieutenant?"

"When can I take her up?"

☆ ☆ ☆

There was one catch to launching the plane. The forty-horsepower engine could fly her but wasn't quite hefty enough to get her off the ground. The plane had to be launched from the back of a flatbed truck at forty-five miles per hour.

At 675 pounds empty, the plane was light enough that Billy could have rolled it onto the truck by himself with a shallow enough ramp, but two of the mechanics rolled it onto the bed nose first and fastened a thumb-release cable to hold it in place until the truck got up to speed.

"You'll feel the lift when the truck hits forty-five. Just trip the release, and you'll be airborne. Good luck."

Billy adjusted his helmet and goggles, one of the few things he was able to bring with him. He tripped the ignition switch and shouted "Contact" out of habit, then reached for the prop. The engine started by manually turning the propeller, like so many older planes. He gave it a spin and the McCullough engine coughed into life.

Billy climbed into the cockpit and slid his feet into the stirrups on the pedals. He worked them and the stick back and forth, then held his hand in a thumbs-up gesture to Gus. Gus signaled the driver, and the truck rolled down the runway.

As the truck picked up speed, Billy felt the plane start to buck, fighting gravity and the tether. As the truck hit forty-five, the driver stuck his arm out the window and gave Billy a thumbs-up. Billy released the catch and the tether fell away. The little plane lifted off the bed and the truck fell behind as Billy opened the throttle and the airplane gathered speed.

Billy pulled back on the stick, and the little plane responded more quickly than his Jenny, owing to its weight and dimensions. He did a few passes around the field, as he felt out the controls, then more confident; he decided to see just what she could do.

Billy did a tight Cuban eight and followed with a series of circular passes, each a little tighter than the one before to determine the plane's minimum radius. So far so good. Time to get serious. He climbed to nearly a thousand feet, then went into a dive. He sighted on the control tower and went into a barrel roll. The plane answered the stick, but when he was coming around from the inverted position, he felt a slight shudder in the left wing. He eased off the throttle and righted the plane. That was a problem for the engineers to solve.

Next, he dipped the plane ninety degrees to starboard and did a perpendicular fly-by, followed by a vertical loop. Again, when the plane went tits up, he could feel the vibration in the left wing. He bottomed out of the loop and swung the plane into a final lazy eight before he came in for a perfect three-point landing.

He taxied to the hangar where Gus and Hennessey were waiting.

"Well, what do you think?"

"She's a sweet little plane. Handles well. I did notice a little bit of vibration in the left wing when I was inverted."

Hennessey shot Gus a look. "That's a glitch we've seen before. The last model we tested showed the same problem, only it was a little more severe. The wing strut broke loose, the wing folded upward and the prop cut it to pieces. The pilot never had a chance to bail out." He turned to Gus. "Get the brains out here. See what they can do about it."

Hennessey turned back to Billy. "Now, Lieutenant, that I've seen you can do what I need you to do, let's go inside and talk about particulars."

"She's a fine machine," Billy said. "I think I'll call her Rosalie."

Gus laughed. "I like that. Up to now the guys called the GA-33 'the Flying Condom'."

Hennessey led Billy into a second story room in a building behind the barracks. The walls and tables were covered with maps. Two men were waiting, lieutenants like himself." Sit down, Lieutenant." Hennessey gestured to a chair. "I can see that you're eminently qualified for the mission, so now I can tell you what it's all about. Have you ever heard of the OSS?"

Billy nodded. "Sure. Who hasn't? Spies, secret agents, I've read a few stories in magazines."

Hennessey gave him a stony stare. "The magazines don't do the truth justice. We have covert operatives in every theater, and many days, bigger battles of the war are conducted undercover than on any battlefield. I have told you previously that we have very valuable asset trapped in occupied France. It is imperative that we get him safely into Allied territory before the end of this week. The most expedient way to do that is to fly him out.

"You and your aircraft will be smuggled into France; you will connect with our agent and fly him and a package that he will be carrying out of France and over the Channel where a carrier will be waiting for you. The hazards are obvious. Have you heard the term 'the Atlantic Wall'?"

Billy shook his head. "No, sir."

One of the other men spoke up. His name tag read Smith, like the other military personnel. "Coastal France is lined with enemy gun emplacements." He spread a map of the area on one of the tables and traced the French coast at the English Channel with his index finger. "Anti-aircraft guns protect all of northern France from air attack over the Channel. Radar monitors the airspace. The Germans call their early-warning system Freya, after the Norse goddess. In addition, Luftwaffe fighter planes are always at the ready to repel invaders. Your advantage lies in the fact that the German defenses are geared to keep people out, not keep people in."

"Sir, I'm not sure about this. Rosalie will only fly at about sixty miles per hour, and from what I've read on the subject, a Messerschmitt fighter will fly at four or five times that speed, at least. Wouldn't a combat pilot have better chance against one of those?"

"We don't want you to fight, soldier, we want you to dodge. Your aircraft will be much more maneuverable because of its size and weight, and the speed you mention will make the Messerschmitts almost clumsy by comparison. They will require far greater space for maneuvering, and if you fly the way I saw you perform at the air show, you can effectively stay out of their line of fire."

One of the other men spoke up, "The Freya radar system is sophisticated, but it's geared for big metal objects, not a small rubber airplane. Also, you'll make a small, very tricky target for the anti-aircraft guns, like shooting a .45 at a house fly. The guns are set up to shoot high altitude targets more than low ones, and if their planes come after you, they won't fire for fear of knocking out one of their own."

"We will also have air cover ready for you if it seems helpful," said Hennessey. "Of course, there is always the possibility that the plane will catch a stray bullet or a lucky shot, but if it does and you have to ditch, you have the comfort of knowing that you have a built in life raft."

"And if the mission fails, what's the backup plan?"

Hennessey stared coldly at Billy. "There is no backup plan. You're it, soldier. Failure is not an option."

Billy thought this over for a minute. "I would make one suggestion to add to the plane, sir."

"What's that, Lieutenant?"

"A rear view mirror."

☆☆☆

Back at the hangar, Gus was tinkering on the left wing strut. "I think I've got the problem solved. Want to take her up again?"

"I want to fly her as much as possible," Billy said. "I'll need to know her like a man knows his wife." His eye drifted to a small rectangular patch on the left wing. "What's that?"

"Just a pinhole leak. Somebody got careless with a screwdriver. It's easy to patch, just like an inner tube. She's made with discrete compartments so that if you take a hit in the fuselage, the wings don't lose air, and vice-versa. The inflation valves are just like the ones in your heart, one-way flow with a flap to prevent loss. She'll take as many as six .30 caliber rounds and still stay airborne if you use the compressor attached to the engine to maintain the pressure."

"I'll take a patch kit with me. I just don't know what good it'll do if I get a bullet hole in the air."

"The answer to that problem is don't get hit."

The second launch from the truck was smoother than the first. Billy had a better feel for the controls and for the plane as a whole. He took it higher this time, pushed it harder, and gained more confidence in the plane and in himself handling it.

He flew over the runway and did his corkscrew finale maneuver. Rosalie performed as well as his Jenny, spiraling smoothly and coming out into a graceful sweeping curve to port. He did a series of tight esses, turning the fuselage almost perpendicular as he did. Small target, fast target, he thought. Keep them guessing.

He circled the field and flew north away from the base toward the mesas he'd seen in his earlier flight. They weren't particularly tall but at least as tall as the buildings on the base, reddish sandstone monoliths that made a series of canyons between them. Billy did a high-level flyover to determine their layout, then he pushed the stick into a dive.

He steered Rosalie between two of the buttes and pulled up sharp when the canyon between them narrowed to a dangerous squeeze. He circled around twice, studying the terrain, and dove again, this time with a plan. As the notch narrowed, Billy tilted the wings almost perpendicular and shot through the gap with a foot to spare between the prop and the landing gear. He shot out of the notch and righted the plane in time to pull up and soar over another mesa that dead ended the corridor.

"Good girl," he said. "Good girl."

He steered west, curious to see how far the desert stretched past the immediate horizon. Two minutes on that course, and the radio crackled. "GA-33, you are flying out of designated airspace. You will be escorted back to the base at once." From the corner of his eye, Billy saw a pair of P-51 Mustangs to port.

And that's how the Army keeps people from stealing their toys, he thought. "Roger that." He dove into a tight 180 and was headed toward the base. Overhead, the Mustangs were slow in coming around. He pulled up on the stick and bobbed up between them, then dove again, sweeping ninety degrees to the right. He climbed and swooped across them, perpendicular to their flight path, his landing gear almost brushing the tops of his pursuers, and darted away again, like crows he'd seen harrying hawks over the farm when he was a boy.

Every time the Mustangs would begin to close on him, Billy would duck or dive or dodge away and leave them playing a less agile catch-up. The radio crackled again. "GA-33, cut the crap. Return to base immediately."

He steered Rosalie between two of the buttes…

"Roger that; just having a little fun. Over and out." Billy tipped his wings in a salute to the Mustangs and flew a straight path to the air field.

He was out of the plane two minutes when Hennessey appeared. "There is a very good reason why you are flying that airplane in the middle of the desert instead of LaGuardia Airport. If you fly out of restricted airspace, there is a good possibility you may be seen by civilians, or worse, by enemy agents. Had you not turned around, standard operating procedure would be to shoot you out of the sky."

"You're serious aren't you?"

Hennessey's silence affirmed the fact.

Gus was deflating the plane. Another mechanic was scrubbing the numbers from the fuselage. It was slowly sagging as if it were melting in the hot sun. "Start practicing," Hennessey told Billy. "You'll need to be able to unpack and ready the GA-33 on your own by tonight. You're flying out at 2300 hours."

Billy spent the next five hours unpacking, inflating, deflating, and repacking Rosalie under Gus's watchful eye, including using a hand pump instead of a compressor. "Just like packing a parachute," he said, "and no less important."

✩ ✩ ✩

That night after supper, Billy and Rosalie were loaded onto another Skytrain with the same crew. He saw that a parachute was attached to a wooden crate that looked like an oversized footlocker holding the airplane. He'd jumped plenty of times with the air show, but he worried that Rosalie might suffer from the experience.

The big risk lay in flying across the Channel. The Atlantic Wall was a formidable barrier. A fighter squadron would create a diversion to open a window for the transport to break through. Either they would make it, or they wouldn't, and Billy would take it from there.

"On the ground, you'll be contacted by members of the Resistance," Hennessey had told him. "They will take you and the aircraft to a safe place to rendezvous with your passenger. His code name is Wormwood."

"Do I have a code name?"

Hennessey thought for a moment and said, "Yes. Four-eyes."

He studied the maps of Normandy and memorized the terrain around Le Havre, the area where he would meet Wormwood and fly him out of France with his mysterious object. The sea cliffs that flanked the harbor were rife with gun emplacements, all aiming out to sea. The plan was to launch Rosalie and fly her up the Seine to its mouth between the cliffs at low altitude and then out to sea where the fighter escort and the carrier would be waiting. All he had to do was dodge the bullets.

Billy tried to sleep, but it was futile. Between the jolting of the C-47 and the combination of excitement and anxiety over the mission, he couldn't close his eyes. In his mind, he rehearsed the assembly and inflation of the plane and the route his flight would take to escape from France.

The Skytrain flew the shortest route, over the North Pole, and the co-pilot brought him a parka with a fur edged hood and a thermos of hot coffee. Outside the window, in the endless daylight of the Arctic Circle, he saw the white ice cap stretching from horizon to horizon. Something to tell my grandkids about, he thought, if I live long enough to have any.

The Skytrain landed in England in the late afternoon their time. A rag-top Land Rover was waiting to take him and the flight crew to a barracks where they would stay until mission time after dark. An RAF sergeant named Parnell was assigned to see to his needs and also to see that he was able, present and accounted for when it was time to fly.

Parnell was a lean man, with an affable grin despite the bad teeth so characteristic of the Brits. His uniform was similar to the U.S. Army's with a few differences; the RAF uniform was a grayish blue and the blouse was belted around the waist. Parnell carried a sidearm in a flap-over holster. A garrison cap and canvas puttees over spit-shined boots completed the uniform.

"Welcome to England, Lieutenant." He pronounced it "leff-tenant." Again, no names.

"I wish I could see more of it," Billy said.

"Perhaps you can come back another time. All the more reason to do well, eh?" Parnell showed him to a single room that was apparently an officer's quarters. The room was Spartan compared to Harper's accommodations, but to Billy, the cot looked heavenly.

"I'll be bringing your supper shortly."

"I'm not eating in the mess hall?"

Parnell shook his head. "My orders are to keep you and your flyboy mates in separate compartments. Can't risk word getting around about your mission, whatever it is. Loose lips and all that."

"You don't know what I'm going to do?"

Parnell put up a hand in a "stop" gesture. "I don't know, and I don't want to know. Better for all concerned that way. Make yourself comfortable, Lieutenant. I'll be back with your supper in a half hour."

Billy wondered what served as standard chow for the RAF. Parnell returned carrying a tray with a napkin over the plate. It smelled pretty good. "With our cook's compliments, his specialty." He swept the cloth away with a flourish. "Stargazey Pie."

Billy stared at the deep dish. The heads of four fish protruded from the golden crust at the compass points, as if they were breaking the surface of a pond. "What the hell is that?"

Parnell grinned. "As I said, Stargazey. It's a pilchard, egg and potato pie. The pilchards are left heads up, as it were, to allow the fish oils to drain under the crust. The heads are looking upward, hence the name Stargazey. It's a sort of superstition we have when someone's off on a dangerous mission. Optimism; looking up, you know."

Billy cocked his head this way and that, studying the alien dish and trying to figure out how he could find it appetizing.

Parnell laughed. "Come in, Corporal." A soldier wearing a cook's apron came in with a tray and set it on the desk.

"We were just having a bit of fun with you, Lieutenant," Parnell said with a chuckle. "That," he pointed at the Stargazey Pie, "is my supper. We prepared this especially for you." The cook uncovered a plate with a steak, baked potato and beans. From a pocket under his apron, the cook pulled a bottle of ale and set it beside the plate.

"Always like to make a chap feel at home," Parnell said. "*Bon appétit.*"

The steak was the best Billy had ever eaten. Maybe it was the way the cook prepared it, and maybe it was the thought that it might be the last one he would ever eat.

✩ ✩ ✩

Billy was dreaming about the farm in Iowa when knocking on the door woke him. He felt that odd disorientation that comes from falling asleep in daylight and waking in darkness. The door opened and the overhead light came on. He put on his glasses and Parnell came into focus. "Time to rise and be ready, Lieutenant."

Billy looked at his watch. He'd only been asleep a few hours, but he felt as if his whole body had shut down. "I need coffee."

"Waiting for you at the plane."

Billy followed Parnell out to the Land Rover where Wilcox and Barnes were waiting. No one spoke as Parnell drove down the airstrip to the C-47.

As they climbed out of the Rover, Parnell said, "I won't jinx you by saying 'good luck,' but you know we're all behind you. What is it you theatre people say to each other? Break a leg?"

"Yep," Wilcox said.

"Right, and amen." He turned to Billy. "Do you have any superstitions, Lieutenant? A good luck charm you carry or some such?"

"I don't believe in luck," Billy said. If anything, "I believe we all make our own."

Parnell grinned. "Right then. Come see us when this mess is over. We'll show you what England's all about, eh?"

"You're on."

They climbed into the Skytrain in the dark, and it was only when the plane was taxied into position that the runway lights came on. The relentless German Blitzkrieg may have ended, but the danger of night raids still loomed large in the British mind. As soon as the plane left the ground, the runway lights snapped off, and it seemed that the plane had suddenly come from nothing and had nowhere to return.

Billy sat in the passenger area, as he had before, but this time, he was wearing a mechanic's coverall and jump boots. A leather helmet capped his head, and he swapped his eyeglasses for his custom made goggles. Five feet away, Rosalie sat near the plane's cargo door, a bulky chute packed neatly top of the crate. He looked at the radium dial of his wristwatch. In less than an hour, he would either be on the ground in France, or be dead.

He reached into a pocket of the coverall and pulled out something Gus had given him back at the hangar. It was a mirror, big as a fifty-cent piece attached to a rod he could clip onto his goggles. "I'd bolt one onto Rosalie," he said with a laugh, "but there's nowhere to drill a hole. The mirror's small, but close to your eye; it'll give you a good field of vision behind you."

From another pocket, he drew a small foil packet. Between his finger and thumb, he felt the oblong shape of what Hennessey called "the last exit," a glass capsule filled with cyanide.

"This has all happened very quickly, and I don't doubt your sense of patriotism or duty," he had told Billy, "but you may have some misgivings about giving your life for this mission. I offer this to you as an option in case you fall into enemy hands. It is a quick death, albeit an unpleasant one, but nothing close to torture at Nazi hands." He added, "Dead men tell no tales."

Gus's advice: don't get shot. Hennessey's advice: don't get caught.

He was given two other items, a regulation .45 caliber automatic painted camouflage green and brown. A lanyard attached the butt of the pistol to a ring on his coverall so it wouldn't get lost when he hit the ground. It's a good thing it's attached, Billy thought, it wouldn't matter if I dropped it in daylight or darkness, I couldn't find it for the camo.

The other was a hooked folding knife to cut his parachute lines if he landed in water or got hung up in a tree. He pressed the button in the handle, and a crescent of razor-edged steel popped out like a hoodlum's switchblade knife. Not exactly reassuring, but there if he needed it.

Nothing to do now but wait, sit back, and listen to the drone of the C-47's engines. He thought about home, Dellville, Iowa, and all the relatives and friends he knew there. They all thought he was crazy for taking up flying, especially with his bad eyes, and crazier for becoming a stunt pilot. Code name "Four-Eyes"; there was another irony. He'd been called that since his grade-school days on the playground. If they could only see him now. The shame of it was, that after the mission was over, he couldn't tell a soul that it happened.

The bitterest pill was Sally Caldwell, the pretty blonde girl who'd sat in the desk in front of him from first grade through high school. She was all gaga over Brad Wooster and promised that she'd wait for him until the war was over, because he joined the Marines the day after Pearl Harbor. He wasn't 4-F, and he didn't wear glasses. Maybe he'd make an exception and tell her. Naah, she wouldn't believe him even if he brought Colonel Hennessey along to swear to it.

The radio crackled in his ear. Wilcox. "Here comes our escort." Billy couldn't hear them , but through the window, he saw the pin point wing lights of three Mustangs flying parallel to the Skytrain. "Lieutenant, get ready. We'll be in the target range within six minutes."

Billy unbuckled his safety belt and slipped his arms into the harness of his parachute. Barnes came back from the cockpit to help him hook the static line from the cargo chute to the stanchion inside the plane. He was just reaching to hook up his own line when bullets ripped through the fuselage.

"Bandits! Three o'clock," Wilcox shouted through the radio. The diversion didn't work. The plane tipped into a hard Starboard dive to evade the fire, and Billy and Barnes staggered to the downside, Barnes crashing against the bulkhead and Billy slamming into him, knocking the wind out of them both.

Wind shrieked through the broken windows. Barnes fought with the lock bar on the cargo door. He dragged it open, and through the open portal, Billy saw the tracers of the dogfight between the Mustangs and the Messerschmitts. He also saw the flames fanning out from the starboard engine over the wing.

"Hook up and jump," Barnes shouted. "We're going to ditch for sure."

"Perry," Billy said, "are we over land yet?"

The radio crackled. "Not for another two minutes at least."

"Wilcox, can you hold it together?"

"Hell, yeah, but I don't know for how long. Cross your fingers."

"Just get us over land," Billy said. "Barnes, help me with the crate." Barnes unbuckled the restraining straps and the pair dragged the crate to the open door just as another burst of machine gun fire raked the plane. Barnes hooked the static line from the crate to the stanchion.

"Thirty seconds," said Perry.

Billy clipped on his static line. Through the cargo door, Billy saw a fireball, but couldn't tell whether it was one of ours or one of theirs.

A blast rocked the plane, as if a giant hand had slapped it. A shell from the cliff side anti-aircraft guns hit the plane between the cargo bay and the tail, ripping a jagged hole in the C-47's skin. The plane jerked violently down then up again.

"Jump!" yelled Barnes, struggling into his chute. "If you wait too long, we'll be too low for your chute to open."

"Not 'til we drop the crate. If it falls in the ocean, the mission's dead."

"If you fall on the ground without a chute, you'll be dead."

"Welcome to France," said Perry. "We're over the target zone."

"Help me," Billy said, putting his shoulder against the crate.

Barnes threw his weight against it, and the crate tipped through the door. The static line went taut, then slack. Barnes grabbed Billy by the shoulders and spun him, throwing him through the door. Billy tumbled head over heels through the darkness then the chute popped and jerked him upright. He groped for the risers. As he drifted down, he saw the flaming C-47 streaking through the sky like a meteor.

Wilcox's voice sputtered through the headset. "Time to bail out, boys. See you on the ground."

Billy would have tried to steer the chute, but below him was total darkness. He pulled his knees as high as he could to roll when he hit, but he never had the chance. He crashed through the branches of a tree and tumbled from limb to limb until he struck his head on one of them, saw, stars, then saw nothing.

✩ ✩ ✩

Billy woke up disoriented. He was upside down in the dark. In the sky, he could hear the sound of engines and gunfire. The dogfight was still going on, so he hadn't been out very long. He groped for the release catch on his harness and hesitated. He could be ten feet off the ground or thirty. With his free hand, he grabbed one of the risers to hold onto instead of falling. He tripped the release.

His body pivoted ninety degrees, and his feet hit the ground in less than a second. He'd been hanging two feet in the air. He wondered about the crew of the Skytrain and hoped they'd all made it out of the plane before it went down. Nothing moved around him.

Billy took a personal inventory and counted himself lucky. He had a knot on his head, but no concussion. He'd had enough of them in his life to recognize the symptoms. No broken bones. Nothing bleeding. He only hoped Rosalie had the same good fortune.

The radio in his helmet was dead. No word in or out. He had to find his allies and dodge his foes on his own ticket. The .45 was some comfort, but it was no match for a German search party with machine guns. He racked a shell into the chamber and hunkered down to wait.

He didn't have to wait long. A light, a thin beam from a lantern bobbed through the brush. If they were Germans, Billy thought, they would have the lights on full to look for him. Hushed voices. They were speaking French.

Billy aimed the .45 toward the light and took the chance. He sang in low tones, "I'll be down to get you in a taxi, honey."

A heavily accented voice responded, "Better be ready 'bout half-past eight."

Billy breathed a sigh of relief and let down the hammer of the automatic with his thumb.

☆ ☆ ☆

The Resistance fighters, Jean and Marcel, led him through the dark forest, across a starlit meadow, and just as a half moon rose over the horizon, to a farm house nested in a grove of trees. Behind it was a barn. To Billy, it looked more like home than he would have imagined.

"Your crate is in there, my friend," Marcel said.

"Then let's get it open and get to work."

"Yes, your passenger may arrive at any time before sunrise, and we should be ready."

Jean opened the barn door and led the way inside by the light of his lamp. Marcel rolled the door closed behind them and threw a switch. A dim electric

Billy aimed the .45 toward the light…

light threw shadows into the stalls and corners.

The crate sat in the middle of the hay-strewn floor. It was scuffed up and splintered in a few places, but seemed intact. Billy put both hands on the crate and his forehead followed. He said the closest thing he knew to a prayer of gratitude and turned to the Frenchmen and said, "Got a crowbar?"

It turned out that Rosalie's wingspan was too wide for the barn door, so the operation moved to the hard-packed dirt outside. Billy had practiced unpacking assembling and inflating the plane many times, but never in the dark. He trusted his instincts and hoped everything was hooked up in the right place. The farm had no air compressor, and the men took turns with hand pumps inflating the wings and fuselage.

"I need a bucket of water and some soap."

Marcel brought the bucket, and while Jean held the lamp, Billy ladled dollops of soapy water over every surface he could. No bubbles, no leaks. The Airmat was intact. A point for Goodyear.

Billy fueled Rosalie from a Jerry can, and she was ready to fly.

Marcel backed an old Citroën flatbed truck up to the airplane and on a pair of planks, the men rolled Rosalie onto the bed. The truck looked as if it might fall apart any second, but Billy could hear under the rattletrap exterior, the sound of a powerful, well-tuned engine.

Billy secured the plane to the bed with the tether cable and things were as ready as they would ever be. Marcel started the truck and pulled across the lane from the barn into an open field. He stopped beside a beehive-shaped hayrick.

The three men each grabbed a pitchfork and began lobbing hay over the truck, covering as much of the plane as the wings would allow. Even in the beam of a spotlight, it would be hard to tell the mound from any other haystack, because the grey rubber of the Airmat blended perfectly into the darkness. Now, all they could do was wait.

"Will we have a long enough straightaway to get your truck to forty-five miles per hour — uh, about seventy-five kilometers— to launch the plane?"

"Don't worry," Jean said. "A short distance from here, the road will allow us to get up to speed. Your people made very clear what is needed." Jean pulled a flask from the pocket of his canvas coat. "I would offer some brandy, but you likely want to keep a clear head, no?"

"Did you ever meet an American who refused a drink, Jean?"

The Frenchman shook his head.

"Well, you still haven't." Jean handed Billy the flask. He saluted his new comrades with it. "Here's to you, and to the mission." He took a long pull, and handed it back.

"And to a brave man," said Marcel, laughing, "willing to fly that, that 'wing-ed' balloon."

And when Billy told them what the mechanics back at base called Rosalie, they all had a good laugh.

Marcel and Jean talked about France and Billy told them about America. The Frenchmen asked about Hollywood and New York City but were the most curious about Baseball and especially about Babe Ruth. "Was he everything we've ever heard he was?" Jean asked.

"All that and more," Billy said. "He's so much of America that I read once that the Japanese soldiers were heard in combat yelling ,'to hell with Babe Ruth,' as an insult."

Marcel nodded. "If my name became a curse to the Nazis, I would consider it the greatest of compliments."

The clock crept into the small hours as the three waited and watched.

"Listen," Marcel said. In the distance, Billy could hear the sound of an engine. Not a car, a motorcycle. It was coming fast.

"Let us hope that this is your passenger." Jean crushed out his cigarette and wrapped the sling of a carbine around his forearm.

The motorcycle roared into the barnyard. The rider shut down the engine. When he pulled his goggles down to hang around his neck, Billy saw a green glow from them. He'd heard of night-vision goggles but had never seen them before.

The rider raised his hands, palms forward.

Marcel sang, "Buy me some peanuts and crackerjack."

"I don't care if I never get back."

"Wormwood." Billy said.

"Four-Eyes. Hail, hail, the gang's all here."

Wormwood stepped off the motorcycle. In the faint light of the moon, Billy could see that the agent was tall and broad-shouldered, but lean and athletic in his build. He was dressed in a light jacket and canvas work trousers. A knit cap on his head completed the look of a Norman peasant.

"Is the plane ready?"

"Yeah."

"Then let's move it. People'll be coming after me any time now."

They pulled away the hay, uncovering the truck and the plane. Billy climbed into the pilot's seat and flipped the ignition switch. "Contact." Wormwood climbed into the passenger compartment. "Strap in," Billy said. "I hope you don't get seasick. Your package secure?"

Wormwood rapped on his chest with his knuckles and Billy heard the solid thump of a metal container. "Secure."

Billy spun the prop, and the McCullough engine stuttered then roared. Billy clambered into the pilot's seat, clipped Gus's mirror onto his goggles, and gave Jean a thumbs-up.

The truck rumbled into life. "*Bonne chance,*" Marcel called out the window, and the Citroën bounced across the field toward the road. It was less than a mile to the straightaway where they could launch the plane, but it seemed like they drove twenty miles over the moonlit landscape before the road stretched before them like a narrow runway.

The truck picked up speed. Rosalie tugged at the cable. Billy watched for Marcel's signal that they were moving fast enough.

"Oh, hell," Wormwood said, reaching over Billy's shoulder to point ahead.

Headlights coming the opposite direction. Billy saw the flash of gunfire, and bullets whanged off the fenders of the truck. Marcel made an executive decision and wrenched the wheel to the left, running the truck into a fallow field in a course at right angles to the road.

Jean levered himself from the passenger seat to sit in the open window, barely hanging on as he shouted, "We're heading toward the sea. Be ready to — a bullet hit Jean, and he tumbled from the window and disappeared under the truck. The rear bucked as the truck ran over his body.

"What was he saying?" shouted Wormwood.

"I think I know."

Two vehicles were chasing the Citroën across the pasture, a truck with men firing at them from the stake side rear, and a car. The truck had better ground clearance and was managing the field better than the staff car; it was gaining on the Citroën.

"The hell with this," said Wormwood. He climbed out of the passenger seat and opened his coat. A Sten machine gun hung under his arm by a braided thong. He emptied most of a clip through the truck's windshield then sprayed the riflemen in the back. The truck cut right sharply and almost hit the rear quarter of the Citroën before its left front wheel dug into a furrow. It flipped quarter-wise and rolled three times before coming to a rest upside down.

The car was still in pursuit, the men at its windows firing pistols. Wormwood rammed another clip into the Sten and fired a burst. One of the car's headlights winked out, but it kept coming.

Marcel honked the horn frantically. Billy, who was watching the gunplay, looked forward. Marcel had flipped on the lights, and Billy saw a hundred feet ahead, a white clapboard fence, and beyond it, blackness. The driver door of the Citroën swung open, and Marcel dived out of it.

"Get in," Billy shouted at Wormwood as the Citroën smashed through the fence and ran headlong over the edge of a cliff. Behind them, the Nazi staff car couldn't stop fast enough and followed it over the precipice. Billy strained his eyes and saw the rocky beach below. He thumbed the release button, Marcel's truck fell away, Billy cracked the throttle, and Rosalie was airborne.

Billy felt a commotion behind him. He looked in his rear view mirror and saw Wormwood's boots sticking out of the passenger seat. "Are you all right?"

"I'm okay," Wormwood's voice said in Billy's ear a few seconds later. "When I saw where we were headed, I dove in the best I could."

"Tap me when you're strapped in."

They were miles east of Le Havre where the Seine reached the Channel, and flying right in front of the Atlantic Wall. He didn't have to worry about radar, but Billy flew low, following the cliffs in the moonlight, lower he hoped than the guns on the cliffs could aim. If their luck held, he could stay out of their sights until he reached the exit zone and would have air cover to get him to the carrier.

Suddenly, the sky lit as bright as day as far down the beach as he could see. The emplacements couldn't fire their guns, but they could fire flares.

Wormwood shouted in his ear. "We got company. Five o'clock high. Two of 'em."

"Hang on to your teeth." Billy yanked the stick and Rosalie peeled away from the cliff just as a spray of bullets ricocheted off its stone face. Rosalie dove within three feet of the water and soared back up in a series of roller-coaster moves to make a harder target. He swung toward the cliffs again, the Messerschmitts in pursuit, and seconds before he would have struck the cliff, he cut the throttle back and swooped upward between his pursuers as the faster planes sped past him.

Billy kept to the cliff. It was a double-edged proposition. On one hand, it gave him cover for one side, but on the other, it limited his options for evasive movement. The Messerschmitts circled and came in from Billy's starboard, hoping to catch him broadside. Billy made a dive that almost planted Rosalie in the sand and peeled away from the cliffs under the fighters.

His eye caught a flicker on one of the gauges. The pressure valve showed a loss. They must have taken a bullet or two in the last volley. He pulled a cable stop and the on-board compressor kicked in.

He rounded a bend in the coast and ahead of him saw a stone formation like an arch jutting from the cliff and into the sea. Beside it was a conical formation projecting almost as high as the cliff. Entretat, he remembered from the maps. He reached under his seat and pulled out a silver canister. "Take this." He handed it over his shoulder to Wormwood. "When I tell you to, pull the ring. It'll get hot, so keep it off the Airmat."

Billy swooped along the cliff in a straight path, inviting pursuit. One of the Germans fell in behind him, angling for a good shot.

"Now."

Wormwood pulled the pin from the canister, and in seconds, white smoke billowed behind Rosalie. Billy threw her into his signature corkscrew, laying down a thick cloud behind him. As he reached the arch, he turned the plane perpendicular. The wingtips barely cleared the opening. Behind him the Messerschmitt, its pilot blinded by the smoke saw it too late. The stone sheared its wings from the fuselage, which plowed into the beach and almost immediately exploded.

Out of the arch, Billy swung into a vertical loop as the remaining fighter fired again. It flew below him at the top of his loop, and he dove at it. "Shoot him." Billy yelled over his shoulder. Wormwood's automatic boomed in Billy's ear as he fired, and bullets spidered the Messerschmitt's canopy glass.

The fighter plane jerked to port as if it were a living thing. The pilot didn't count on being a target himself. Billy looped, and this time when the Messerschmitt came at him, he flew at it head on. Wormwood shoved another clip into his automatic, and Billy handed back his .45. "Take him down."

Before the German pilot could fire, Billy wrenched the stick and brought Rosalie around in a tight figure-eight to sweep past the Messerschmitt at a forty-five degree angle, leaving its fuselage an easy target.

Wormwood shot rapid fire with both hands like a Wild Bill Hickock on the cover of a dime novel. The Messerschmitt weaved crazily and then disappeared like a silver wraith into the sea.

Billy swung Rosalie north on the bearing for the carrier. He was almost sighing with relief when an explosion burst above him at ten o'clock. He dove as more shells exploded in the air. The pressure gauge was fluttering lower. Shrapnel must have torn the Airmat, he thought. He cranked up the compressor and crossed his fingers.

The wings were staring to flap slightly, and Billy could feel Rosalie losing stability. He realized that his best bet to reach the carrier was to hold his heading and fly a straight path, but he also knew that if he did, the gunners would find their trajectory and he and Wormwood were dead men.

He began a slalom pattern, cutting banked esses and bobbing up and down. They might have to ditch, but their prospects were a lot better if they lived to hit the water. He cut their airspeed as much as he possibly could to take the strain off the wings. The sea was only twenty feet below them now.

Ahead, he saw a flare rocket into the sky. It was the carrier, a mile, maybe a mile and a half away, but Billy felt the plane softening around him, and as a last desperate move, he pulled back full on the stick. The nose jerked up sharply, like a horse at a tug of its bridle. The rear of the plane plowed the water, throwing a rooster tail of spray behind it, and the fuselage pitched forward, hydroplaning over the whitecaps.

Rosalie came to rest, bobbing on the waves like an exhausted seagull.

"You okay?" Wormwood said.

"Yeah, I'm okay."

"Fire a flare. let them know where we are."

No sooner did Billy fire his signal than bullets pocked the water near them. More German fighter planes. They swung for a second pass and strafed Rosalie. Billy cried out in pain.

"I'm hit. My leg."

"We've got to get away from the plane. Come on, pull yourself out of the cockpit and I'll take it from there."

Billy dragged himself from the pilot's seat almost in shock from the wound. Wormwood pulled him to his chest and began paddling away from Rosalie with his free hand. "Hang on, Four-Eyes. I'll get us out of this." Wormwood's voice sounded far away, like he was shouting down a drainpipe. The stars over head became watery and dim.

The Germans swooped down for another run. Their engines snarling like a chorus of doom. In the distance, Billy heard thunder, and overhead, the first plane exploded in a scarlet ball of flame. A shell exploded near the second fighter, and it swerved away only to be tagged by another shot from the carrier's guns. The third plane turned tail and flew in the general direction of safety.

"Hang on, Four-Eyes. They're coming for us now."

"Billy," he muttered, "Not Four-Eyes. Billy." He closed his eyes and drifted into the merciful arms of sleep.

Billy woke a little bit at a time. The first thing that woke was his head, which ached from the lump he'd taken falling through the tree. Then, gradually consciousness worked its way down his torso, finally waking the throbbing pain in his left leg. Without his glasses, the room was a grey blur. Was the bed rocking, or was he woozy from the IV bottles plugged into his arm? Oh yeah, the carrier. He was on a ship.

Someone hooked his glasses over his ears, and he found himself staring into Wormwood's face. "Hello—Billy."

"Where are we?"

"Almost to Liverpool."

"You're okay. How about the package?"

Wormwood rapped on his chest. "Under my shirt."

"All that action and you can't tell me what it is, huh?"

"Rules are rules. I can't *tell* you but no rule says I can't let you *see* it. You deserve that much. You damn near died on this mission." Wormwood stood and closed the door to the corridor. He unbuttoned his shirt.

Across his chest, Billy saw tattoos; not the usual eagle or girlfriend's name, but odd geometric figures, bits of foreign languages, and symbols. Wormwood worked the catches on the case. Maybe the morphine made him see things, but when the case opened, the tattoos seemed to glow a dull red, like embers in a fire place. The inside of the case was lined with what looked like lead.

What wormwood drew from the case was two pieces of glass clamped together over what looked like a hand-sized patch of very thin leather covered with symbols arranged like a paragraph. In the center of the fine blue script was a withered nipple. Through the glass, Billy saw that Wormwood's tattoos now glowed yellow like metal on a blacksmith's forge.

"What—what is it? I mean, I know what it is, sort of, but what's it mean?"

"It means we have a better chance of winning the war now that we have it and the Nazis don't." He put the artifact back into the case, and the glow of his tattoos faded. As he buttoned his shirt, Wormwood said, "And I can tell you that if you hadn't gotten me out of France and to this ship, we'd all be a whole lot the worse for it."

He rose from his chair, and started for the door.

"Wait—I don't even know your name."

Wormwood paused at the threshold. "You deserve that, too. It's Randall, Billy." He reached into a pocket of his trousers and pulled out a dull brassy coin. He held it between his thumb and forefinger, studying it for a moment, then pressed it into Billy's palm. "Keep this. It's always brought me luck, and it'll do the same for you."

"I never believed in luck."

"I never believed in luck before, either, or in magic. War changes your perspective."

"You saved my life out on the water."

"Yeah, I guess I did," Randall said with a chuckle. "The Chinese have a saying that if you save a man's life, you're responsible for whatever he does afterward. I don't think you'll disappoint me, Billy. We probably won't meet again, so, have a good life."

"Goodbye—Randall." And he was gone.

✩ ✩ ✩

The trip home was on a troop carrier out of Liverpool.

"Uncle Sam seems in a sweat to get you to the battle, but takes his good old time sending you home," a soldier on crutches like Billy's grumbled, as they jostled in the chow line. "Priorities," he snorted. "Damned priorities."

Billy decided to not tell him that after the hectic days he'd spent on his mission, he was happy to have a few routine ones with no excitement or worries, if he overlooked the possibility of the ship hitting a mine or being torpedoed by a German U-Boat.

Stateside, the Army gave him two things, discharge papers and a train ticket to Dellville, Iowa. He spent the next two days staring out the windows of the passenger car, just glad to be back in the U.S. again.

The farm hadn't changed, but it never did. His parents were happy to see him, once they finished scolding him about his injury and telling him more than once that they warned him that if he kept doing crazy stunts, he'd end up hurting himself. Billy took it and didn't argue. If they believed he was hurt working the air show, so much the better.

Three days after he came home, an olive drab staff car with white stars and numbers on the doors bumped down the lane to the farm, throwing a cloud of dust in its wake. Billy was sitting on the porch when it pulled up into the yard, setting the dogs to barking. The back door opened, and Colonel Hennessey stepped out.

Billy's parents came out of the house as Hennessey climbed the steps to the porch. Billy pulled himself to his feet with the crutch. "Colonel." He nodded a greeting. "What brings you all the way out here?"

Hennessey's eyes drifted to Billy's mother and father. "Could we talk, privately, Lieutenant?"

His parents looked at each other. "It's okay, Mom, Dad."

They went inside, but Billy could see them peering through the lace curtains of the parlor. Hennessey looked around him before he spoke. "You know, son, I envy you. You'll always have this to come home to. The Army is my home, and I have nowhere else to go." He reached into his pocket and pulled out a small manila envelope.

"Hold out your hand." Billy did. "There was some argument over who had priority, the Congress or the Army. Since you were on active duty when you performed your service to the Country, the Army won, so instead of a Congressional Gold medal, you're getting this." He tipped the envelope and two medals fell into Billy's palm; one a Purple Heart, and the other a medal on a blue ribbon edged with red and white.

The second medal was an ornate bronze cross with a spread eagle at its center. Below the eagle, a scroll bore the words, "For valor." He turned it over and found inscribed on the back: Lt. William T. Chadwell.

"Since officially, the mission never happened, Command felt that a ceremony would be inappropriate, so this will have to do." Hennessey snapped to attention, and saluted Billy. Billy returned the salute. Hennessey turned on his heel.

He was almost off the porch when Billy said, "Colonel." Hennessey halted and turned. "Tell Gus that the strut held. He fixed it right." Hennessey nodded. He stepped off the porch and within a minute, the olive green Ford was kicking up dust in the other direction.

Billy sat for a while on the porch, staring at the medals. His mother and father came back out and sat in chairs on either side of him. They stared at the medals too. The Distinguished Service Cross; it was the highest award short of the Congressional Medal of Honor. He reached into his pocket and pulled out the dull brass coin Randall had given him. He rubbed one thumb over the runes on the coin and the other over the eagle on the medallion.

"Son," his father said, "We don't know what it is you done, and maybe we never will, but we're proud of you."

As soon as he could drive, Billy decided, he would make a trip into town, or maybe just have Dad take him. He had a call to pay on Sally Caldwell. Maybe with luck, his medal, and the intriguing mystery of a top secret mission, she just might give Four-Eyes another look.

THE END

A 4-F HERO

When Ron told me he needed an airplane adventure story, I saw it as a real challenge. Serendipity struck, as it often does, and I happened to see a show about the OSS and its experimental weapons in World War II. One of them was an inflatable airplane. According to the documentary, it was shelved because it was too hazardous for the pilot, but I found the idea intriguing.

The military and intelligence community exhaust every bit of technology for war and espionage purposes before you and I are allowed to know it exists, so it's no stretch to believe that the inflatable airplane was up and running on a covert mission.

My original idea was to have C. O. Jones (code name Wormwood in the COJ novels) use it to escape occupied Europe after succeeding in some mission, but when the air adventure anthology emerged, I decided to put the focus on the plane and pilot, make C.O. Jones the rescuee, and make Chadwell the main character. As it stands, the story fits in with the C.O. Jones series of novels, but Wormwood doesn't steal the show from Billy.

Billy, a 4-F, doesn't let his handicap prevent him from doing what he loves to do: fly. He is a daredevil stunt pilot with a barnstorming air show, and who better to fly a plane for the sake of evasion than a stunt pilot.

I had Colonel Hennessey, C. O. Jones's boss, impress Billy into service under the cloak of the OSS for his unique flying skills and turn him loose to fly by the seat of his pants, literally and figuratively in a dangerous mission in a dangerous plane.

I had great fun playing "what-if" with the plane and the situation. What could go wrong? A lot, and most of it did, but between Billy and Wormwood, they pulled it off. The story is set a year before D-Day, but the details of the Atlantic Wall, contemporary aircraft, experimental planes, the Dry Lake test field , the inflatable plane, and the Entretat arch and needle are all for real.

If you're curious about the Goodyear Inflataplane, Google it, and you'll find declassified film footage and even an episode of the old I've Got A Secret TV show in which the blindfolded panel asks questions of an officer while he inflates the plane in the studio in front of them.

A real kick in the story for me was having a four-eyed, 4-F kid like me rise to meet the challenge of heroism and duty and come out the other side alive, respected by the best of the best, even if he can't tell his friends and neighbors; fighting bad guys back to back with a class A bad ass and winning. I loved to read stories like that when I was a kid, and I had a ball writing this one.

FRED ADAMS - is a western Pennsylvania native who has enjoyed a lifelong love affair with horror, fantasy, and science fiction literature and films. He holds a Ph.D. in American Literature from Duquesne University and recently retired from teaching writing and literature in the English Department of Penn State University. He has published over 50 short stories in amateur, and professional magazines as well as hundreds of news features as a staff writer and sportswriter for the now Pittsburgh Tribune-Review. In the 1970s Fred published the fanzine *Spoor* and its companion *The Spoor Anthology. Hitwolf, Six-Gun Terrors* and *Dead Man's Melody* were his three first books for Airship 27, and his most recent novel for Airship 27 is *C. O. Jones: the Damned and the Doomed.*

Clippers of the Clouds

In the early 20th Century, German Count Ferdinand von Zeppelin pioneered the creation of rigid, lighter-than-air craft capable of long distance flights. During World War One they were adapted for military use as long range bombers wreaking havoc upon Great Britain from their lofty positions high above the clouds where fixed-winged fighters could not reach them. After the war, Zeppelins became pleasure ships utilized in luxury Trans-Atlantic Flights and were highly popular.

The Golden Era of the airship was the 1930s, the same period as that of the pulps and it is no surprise their romantic images would inspire pulp writers of the time. The original monthly, ZEPPELIN STORIES, was produced solely to highlight these magnificent flying machines in exciting, colorful and fast-paced adventures. Now, Airship 27 Productions, itself bearing the image of these high-flying cruisers, launches a brand-new series devoted to airships.

In this debut volume you will thrill to the exploits of Jim Beard's new hero, Tracer Talbot, as he encounters a mysterious pirate airship and her crew. While writer I.A. Watson sets off on an aerial adventure aboard an experimental Zeppelin built to explore the skies of an alien dimension. Join us as AIRSHIP 27 – ZEPPELIN TALES Volume One soars into the stratosphere of the imagination on this, its maiden flight.

Zeppelin Tales
VOLUME ONE

AN AIRSHIP 27 PRODUCTION

AIRSHIP27HANGAR.COM

NEW PULP

PULP FICTION FOR A NEW GENERATION!

FOR AVAILABILITY OF THIS AND OTHER FINE READING: AIRSHIP27HANGAR.COM

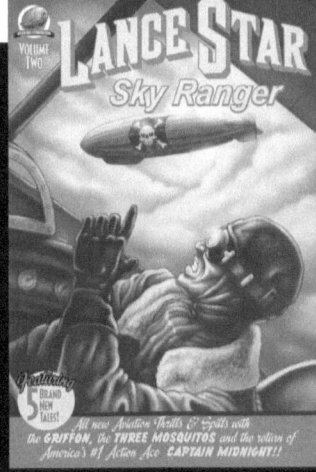